Peter Reese Doyle

PUBLISHING

Colorado Springs, Colorado

TRAPPED IN PHARAOH'S TOMB

Copyright © 1993 by Peter Reese Doyle

Library of Congress Cataloging-in-Publication Data
Doyle, Peter Reese, 1930-
    Trapped in Pharaoh's Tomb / Peter Reese Doyle.
        p. cm— (Daring Adventure Series)
    Summary: Mark and Penny Daring and their friend David Curtis
are helping to translate ancient writing in a newly discovered
tomb in Egypt. After they discover great treasures, they are
trapped and just barely find their way out through a secret tunnel
to the Nile.
    ISBN 1-56179-143-1
[1. Egypt—fiction.] I. Title. II Series: Doyle, Peter Reese,
1930- Daring Family Adventure Series.

Published by Focus on the Family Publishing, Colorado Springs,
Colorado, 80995

Distributed by Word Books, Dallas, Texas

Edited by Etta Wilson
Cover illustration by Ken Spengler
Cover design by James A. Lebbad

Printed in the United States of America

    94 95 96 97 98/ 10 9 8 7 6 5 4

For

Sally Ann

With inexpressible gratitude and love.

CONTENTS

CHAPTER 1

BURIED ALIVE

The massive stone door of the tomb slammed shut with a sound like a terrific explosion! Shock waves reverberated down the airtight chamber and rebounded off the far wall. The long entrance hall was plunged into darkness!

Standing beside that wall, Mark Daring, his sister Penny, and David Curtis whipped around in alarm, shocked by the sudden crash. Their ears were stunned by the dreadful sound. They looked toward the tomb entrance, but they saw nothing but blackness. Now their only light came from the two battery-powered lamps that illuminated the walls they'd been photographing. That light seemed no more than a faint spark against the ocean of darkness engulfing them.

"Wait here!" David shouted, racing to his pack, which was propped against the wall. He grabbed a flashlight and dashed through the blackness, sprinting after the yellow beam that sliced the dark void ahead of him. His ears still hurt from the thunderous shock of the crashing door; his heart pounded wildly.

"Be careful, David!" Penny called after him.

Her brother Mark rushed to his own pack and pulled

out a flashlight. "I'll turn out one of these lanterns," Mark said, "to save the batteries." Then the powerfully built young man put his arm around his slender sister. Even in the dim light from the remaining lamp, Mark could see the anxiety in her face.

Above and around them on every side, the varicolored hieroglyphics and paintings leered ominously down, sinister in the artificial light. Penny tore her eyes away from the large crocodile-faced figure that towered on the wall beside her and shuddered as she buried her face in her brother's shoulder.

"What happened, Mark?" she cried.

"The tomb door slammed shut, Penny," he replied soberly.

They both knew that the huge stone door blocked the only way out of the tomb—a tomb buried deep in desert sand.

"But it's so heavy it takes three men to open and close it," she answered. "How could it have shut by itself?"

Mark was alarmed as well, but he knew they dared not panic. "Maybe the men were working with the door and let it slip," he ventured. But he didn't believe that and she knew it.

David ran through the blackness of the hall and reached the door whose sudden closing had trapped the three of them in the tomb. The great stone slab rested on hinges cut into the massive blocks that formed the wall. The door and its frame sloped inward toward the top. To close it, at least three men on the outside had to lift it before letting it fall shut. There was *no way* that it could close by itself.

David shined his powerful light along the edges of the yellow stone door, which seemed to be an airtight fit against the wall in which it was set.

Maybe there's a crack for air, he said to himself. Switching off his light, he looked again around the stone surface. But there were no cracks, no sign of light from the outside. The door fit too perfectly into the wall.

He shouted—but no one answered. He struck the door with the flat of his hand—but quit that in a hurry. He could only hurt himself striking that solid stone.

Frantically, he loosened the laces of his boot, yanked it off, and pounded the heel against the door. Again and again he struck the massive stone slab, hoping someone would hear. There was no reply. Now he knew their situation was very serious. They had to find air.

The tomb had been built four thousand years ago. Through the centuries, however, the desert winds had covered it completely with sand; it had been lost to human memory. The only entrance that had been opened so far was the sloping tunnel from the surface down to the tomb door that was now deep underground. That door had just slammed shut!

Yet surely those who'd shut it had known what they were doing—and would open the door quickly! Paul Froede had lectured them on the hazards of their work, and on the importance of keeping the doors of the rooms in which they worked open. "We've had no time to examine this tomb yet," he'd told them, "and we don't know if there's any ventilation. Keep the doors open and your flashlights handy—just in case."

Knowing it was futile, David nevertheless put his light in his pocket, placed his back against the massive stone, and tried to shove it open. It didn't budge. Now David felt a hopelessness he'd never known. There was no light, there was no sound from the other side. The temperature inside the buried tomb was quite cool, but David felt the sweat running down his body, causing his khaki shirt to cling to his broad, muscled back.

Turning, he saw his friends seventy feet away, standing forlornly in the tiny arc of light from Mark's lamp on the floor. Penny stood close beside the solid bulk of her brother, held in his protective arm.

Switching his flashlight on, David followed its beam quickly back through the engulfing darkness. The light from the lantern beside Penny and Mark was lost in the high-ceilinged blackness of the weirdly decorated ancient chamber.

Even though David was six feet, one inch tall and Mark only two inches shorter, the darkness made the three of them feel like pygmies lost in a giant's hall; pygmies surrounded by the dangerous animals, alligator-men, serpents, and sinister gods that marched around them on every wall.

"The door won't budge," David told them. "There's

no sound from the other side. I guess the stone's too thick to hear through. When I turned off the flashlight, I couldn't see any daylight around the door. It must be airtight—like Mr. Froede said."

Penny's heart was pounding, but she kept her voice calm. "But who closed the door?" she asked. "Mr. Froede told everyone how important it was to leave all the doors open. What could have happened?"

"I don't know," David replied. Penny thought his dark hair looked black in the dim light thrown up by the lantern, his lean face deeply troubled.

"They'll open it pretty soon," Mark said hopefully. "We know they're not going to leave us here. Mr. Froede'll be here in a minute."

"What if he isn't?" Penny asked, looking up into his shadowed face.

"But what would stop him?" Mark tried to smile reassuringly at his sister.

"What would stop him? The same thing that made it possible for someone to shut the door in the first place," she answered. "Mr. Froede would never have closed the tomb without telling us. I think he's in trouble."

Then David had a sudden thought. "Penny, why don't you like Ahmet? You told us from the beginning that you weren't sure about him. What made you say that?" David didn't know why he asked the question, but maybe it had something to do with the danger they were in now. Neither he nor Mark had understood Penny's suspicions about the Egyptian.

Ahmet was Mr. Froede's foreman, the man who managed the Egyptian team that was excavating and exploring this newly discovered tomb. A tall, exceedingly friendly man, he'd won over the boys from the day they'd met him. But Penny distrusted him for some reason, and had mentioned it to both boys two days ago.

When she didn't answer, David repeated his question. "Why don't you like him?"

Mark and David looked at the slender girl whose face was half in shadow. They could see that she was perplexed. "I don't know . . . " she replied haltingly. "I just don't feel we can trust him."

"But he's the guy in charge of the whole work crew," Mark said, puzzled by her attitude. "If we can't trust him, who can we trust?"

No one answered.

Mark and David looked at each other over Penny's head, their minds racing. Her life was now in their hands.

The only sound that broke the centuries-old stillness was that of their own breathing.

Penny broke the silence. "What can we do?" She sounded forlorn.

"First, we've got to find air," Mark answered quickly, "before we run out!"

The darkness closed on them with all the weight of the massive stone building above their heads. The four-thousand-year-old pharaoh's tomb had just become their grave!

CHAPTER 2

FLIGHT TO EGYPT

Just four days earlier, Mark, Penny, and David had flown into Cairo with Mr. Froede, a close friend of Mark and Penny's father. They'd had a glorious flight over spectacular African scenery, flying in the luxurious Gulfstream IV from East Africa, where Mark and Penny lived, to the capital of Egypt. The magnificent corporate jet belonged, Froede had told them, to the French-German corporation for which his firm worked. He had used it to pick them up and to bring back some special equipment from the mining company where the Darings lived.

Paul Froede and Mr. Daring owned a firm that had been working in Egypt for the past seven years. They'd done mining surveys for the Egyptian government as well as for foreign firms. They were uniquely qualified to study underground formations—and buried buildings.

David was visiting the Darings for the summer from the States. He had become involved in this adventure when Mr. Froede had persuaded their parents to let the three teens come to Egypt and help with translation work for the firm.

On the plane Froede had not spoken much about the

translation work the three teens would be doing on this special project; instead, he'd pointed out the stunning African scenery over which they were flying. Immense waterfalls, deep gorges, gushing rivers, wide grasslands, desolate lava plateaus—he seemed to recognize them all. He was a fascinating tour guide and a gifted storyteller, and he'd kept them engrossed for hours.

When they arrived in Cairo late that afternoon, Froede whisked them through customs and then into the company car which was waiting outside. He drove them to his one-story home, where his wife, Joan, met them with open arms. A tall, dark-haired woman, she'd known Mark and Penny for years—since they were little, in fact. The Darings and the Froedes were old friends.

"You'll stay with us tonight and tomorrow night as well," Mrs. Froede told them as she led Penny to her room. Then she took the boys to the room they would share. "You can unpack and wash up, and then Paul wants to talk about the work you'll be doing with him. We'll have supper at six."

A short while later, they were seated with Mr. Froede in his study, drinking cold Perrier. David stared fascinated at the bookshelves that lined the dark panelled walls. A deep red Persian carpet covered the floor. Brass lamps stood by the sofa, and there was one on the desk as well.

He sat beside Penny on the sofa across from Froede's desk, while Mark perched on the edge of a chair to their right. The windows were closed, the curtains drawn, and an air conditioning unit was humming in the window.

Mr. Froede's round red face topped a well-proportioned body. A vigorous man, he exuded energy even when sitting.

"Let me turn this on before I begin," Froede said mysteriously. He opened a drawer in his desk and flipped a switch. Noticing the boys' questioning faces, he grinned, a twinkle in his eye, and said, "This little machine scrambles sound and makes it hard for anyone to listen in on our conversation from a car parked on the street."

David and Mark exchanged glances. *Why would anyone want to listen to what went on in Mr. Froede's home?* This job might be more exciting than they'd realized.

"All right!" Froede said decisively. "You three have been very patient with me the whole day. Not even Penny has asked any questions about the project!" He flashed her a broad smile.

Penny flushed. "Uncle Paul!" she said indignantly. Then she laughed.

"I realize you want to know what your father and I are up to in Cairo. And what you'll be doing here." He grinned slyly at Penny and the boys. "What we've found is incredible," Froede began, his blue eyes gleaming with excitement in his flushed face. "No one's uncovered this tomb before—not even the robbers who've found almost all the other great treasures in Egypt. As far as we can tell, this one is practically untouched."

He jumped up and strode across the floor in front of them. "And our company has the contract from the Egyptian government to work with the French-German organization that's doing the excavating! Originally, you see, we thought we were working on something else entirely.

"Several years ago we were doing preliminary investigations on a site where the government planned to build an observatory when our instruments detected this huge complex of buildings underground. We kept this absolutely secret—as our agreement with the Egyptians required—and only two men in the government department we work with were told about it."

He paused. "And no one on my team knew either, except Keno. So I handled the equipment that mapped this tomb." He stopped and looked at each of them in turn, then stabbed his finger at Mark. "This is vital—you must not talk about this to anyone but me!"

Mark moved to the edge of his chair. "But why did it take so long to start excavating if you found it several years ago?" he asked.

"You can't imagine the restrictions the government has about such things," Froede replied. "Egypt has had so many of its ancient treasures stolen by foreigners—and by foreign governments—that they've made it almost impossible for such work to begin without iron-clad government control."

He sat down in his chair and drummed his fingers on the desk. "Our contact man in the Egyptian government had a very difficult task: to clear this work through the right channels without letting it be known what we'd actually found! We, or rather, our contacts in the government office we work with, had to secure release from the restrictions regarding ancient buildings, while we pretended to be preparing the site for an observatory."

"This find is fantastic!" He pounded the desk but quit when his coffee cup rattled dangerously. "It was built four thousand years ago, but lost to sight when the weather patterns changed and mounds of sand smothered the area. Whole cities were obliterated, in fact. Vast cultivated areas were simply covered and lost to human knowledge for centuries."

He rummaged among the papers on his desk. "Look at this sketch of the structure we've found. It contains a king's tomb, but there's more . . . but I'll explain that later. Here, look at these." He jumped up, came around the desk, and handed Penny computer-generated drawings of the underground complex.

Mark left his chair and knelt beside her, while David moved closer on her other side. The outline of the tomb was measured in meters, and the various heights of the building's components were printed beside each section. The dimensions were astounding.

"You mean the entire tomb has been covered with sand all these centuries, and no one knew it?" David asked. His dark brown eyes gleamed with excitement. This was the real project Mr. Froede had brought them to Egypt to work on!

"That's right," Froede replied. "It's sealed airtight. Rather, it *was* sealed."

Penny put down her glass of Perrier. "Have you uncovered any of the buildings yet?" she asked.

"Not yet," Froede replied. "We've dug an entrance below the ground and slanted a tunnel down to the main door, but we've done nothing to uncover the building except open the front hall. We want to map and explore the whole place before we let the news out. Once we do that, we'll have to cope with mobs of press people and adventurers—and thieves—who will flock to such a find."

He sipped his coffee, then put down the cup, jumped up, and paced the room. Excitedly he told how they'd found the building with their instruments, located the entrance, and dug a sloping tunnel down to it. "Listen, you three! Tomorrow I'm taking you to the museum to see the kind of treasures ancient Egyptian craftsmen made. I've got an appointment with the director. While I meet with him, you'll be able to see the things they've taken out of the pharaohs' tombs. That's what we'll uncover when we get into this one! This is the excavation of the century!" His bright blue eyes gleamed with excitement.

"But Uncle Paul," Penny asked wonderingly, "why do you and Dad need our help? Surely you could get other translators, real professional ones: I mean, who'd do a better job than we could."

He turned and faced her. "Perhaps we could, Penny, but we don't want to! You three are friends—not professionals. You won't be noticed, but any new translators we hire in this city might be. Our employers in Europe urged us to keep a very low profile. We can't give any indication that we're on to anything special.

"Besides," he continued, looking directly at Mark and Penny, "I've known you for years. Your father and I trust you completely—and David, as well!" He grinned at David, who grinned back modestly.

Froede paused a moment, then added, "And there's another reason. Your dad and I thought you'd have fun doing preliminary work on this excavation Later we will have professionals come in to finish the work. He said you three had earned it." He beamed at them as they took in his words, and then turned back to his desk. "Here's what you're going to do."

They listened, entranced, as he told how they would move with him to the tomb site in the desert and live in a trailer. A small crew was there, guarding the tunnel to the tomb and waiting for his return. The key to their work was an Egyptian named Keno.

"You'd never pronounce his last name, so don't try. He wants us all to call him 'Keno'. He can *sight read* the hieroglyphics we've found inside the tomb hall." Froede sighed and shook his head in wonder. "The man's a genius with languages!"

He continued to explain how they would enter the tomb, proceed down the entrance hall, and let Keno read the markings on the wall and translate them into English. The hieroglyphics described the buildings and the burial chamber. From what he'd already read, Keno knew they gave directions for entering the other rooms.

"You, Penny, will photograph the sections of the wall as Keno translates. You, David, will translate from his English into German, on a microcassette recorder I'll give you. And you, Mark, will do the same in French."

He paced the room again, then stopped in front of Penny. "You, Young Lady, will also be our secretary! Keno will speak his English translation into a microcassette recorder After supper, while Mark and David are revising their translations into more polished French and German, you'll play back Keno's tape and type that into your lap-top." He grinned at her again: "Now you know why your dad told you to bring the thing! You thought you were taking too much equipment - and too few clothes - didn't you?"

He smiled at Penny, and she smiled happily back. *What an adventure!* she thought, her brown eyes shining. Glancing quickly at David and Mark, she saw that they were as excited as she was!

Froede called Penny's attention back with his instructions. "You'll use floppy disks—not just your hard drive. A machine is too easily stolen! You'll make one disk copy for me and one for the head office in Europe. And, as I said, you're also the photographer. We'll develop your negatives in our trailer and then send them to Paris with the tapes the boys have made.

"The men in Paris want these tapes and pictures right away! There's a stone in the Louvre with hieroglyphics from the same period as those we've found in this tomb. It was probably carried off by one of the adventurers who plundered Egypt in the last century, and somehow it found its way to France. That piece gives directions to the tomb rooms. The men in Paris will send us pictures of their piece of the same stone; then we'll match them to pictures we have of the main piece here in the museum in Cairo. All these directions together should give us the information we need to begin to really explore this tomb complex.

"Meanwhile, we've got plenty to do! Tomorrow we'll visit the museum and you can see the main piece. It's just like having a map of the whole complex— except the treasure rooms. We think we'll find the rest of the information on the stone in Paris. Apparently, the stones hold the original architect's plans."

He slapped his fist into his palm. "There's only a handful of people in the world who can read these hieroglyphics—our man Keno is one of them. But he needs pictures of the stone in the Louvre before he can lead us to the treasure rooms."

Froede frowned. "The folks in Paris are trying to get permission to photograph that stone. With that information and the pictures and tapes we send them, they can also check Keno's rough translation. But someone in the Louvre is dragging his feet—for reasons we don't understand—and they haven't yet taken those pictures."

He was silent for a moment; he seemed hesitant to express his suspicions. Obviously, there was something mysterious going on and it troubled him, but all he said was, "There seems to be some dirty work afoot."

For a moment Froede stood before them lost in thought. Then he snapped back to the present and began to pace the room again. "When we locate the treasure, the Egyptian government will then be able to remove it to a safe place." He continued to pace before them. "There's a fortune down there. It's beyond calculation! And *we'll* be the ones to discover it!"

The three teens were trying to digest all this information when Froede suddenly stopped his vigorous pacing and stood motionless before them. He looked at each in turn. They waited, breathless in the tense atmosphere.

Then he broke the spell. "So how does it sound? Do you want to do it?"

"Yes, sir!" the three exclaimed in unison.

"Time for supper!" Mrs. Froede called.

CHAPTER 3

THE EGYPTIAN ANTIQUITIES MUSEUM

Mark and David rose early the next morning, dressed quickly in shorts and T-shirts, and went quietly out the back door to the enclosed yard behind Froede's house. They needed exercise!

"Man, I'm stiff after that day in the plane!" Mark complained, as they both began to jog in place.

It was early but Cairo was already alive; the boys could hear cars going by the house. Although the Froedes lived in a suburb of the city, the honking of car horns and the sound of buses reminded them that they were surrounded by fourteen million people!

"We're going to have to stay in shape this trip, Mark," David replied. "I've got a premonition of something! I think this job is bigger than we thought. I bet it's even bigger that Mr. Froede thought!"

David had been pondering their conversation with Mr. Froede the day before. Several things had sounded

17

weird. David didn't want to imagine trouble where there wasn't any, but he did want to ask Mark if he'd picked up the same suspicions. "What do you think Mr. Froede meant when he told us there was 'dirty work afoot' in the Louvre?"

Both boys were sweating now as they continued running in place. Mark's broad, friendly face gleamed as he replied, "That puzzled me too. Does he think that other people have found out about this tomb, that they're trying to keep Mr. Froede's crew from getting the information they need?"

The boys thought about this for a few minutes, but then forgot the matter as they finished their calisthenics and began karate exercises. They liked to spar with each other. Mark was heavier and stronger; David taller and faster. But they were both well trained and evenly matched.

Finally they cooled down, went inside, and showered. When they came to the breakfast room, Penny was already dressed and eating breakfast with the Froedes. She and Mrs. Froede were laughing at something Mrs. Froede had said.

"Sit down, boys," Mrs. Froede said, getting up and going into the kitchen. She came back with eggs, fruit, bread, and a pitcher of milk. "Help yourself. There's more if you want it."

"Oh, they'll want it, Mrs. Froede," Penny said. "They're real hogs when it comes to food! That's why Dad gave me a check to give you." Penny looked seriously at their hostess, but her eyes twinkled. "Dad's afraid the boys will eat you into bankruptcy! He said to tell you that the boys are *basically* good—he thinks—they just have this problem with food."

She smiled a sad, pitying smile at David and Mark. "The Bible calls it 'gluttony', Dad says, and he worries about them. Gluttony's a spiritual problem, according to the Bible, and Dad doesn't want them to get fat like Eli did." She looked at the boys across the table, mock concern clouding her pretty brown eyes.

Neither Mark nor David could answer her—their mouths were full! Froede laughed out loud at the looks on their faces. "Eat up, you two!" he encouraged. "These women don't mind our stuffing ourselves—not as long as it puts muscle on us so we can protect them!"

Mark and David looked daggers at Penny as they continued to eat a *very* healthy breakfast. She smiled back innocently.

When the boys had finished, Froede jumped up. "We leave for the museum in ten minutes," he said, striding vigorously from the room.

"Let me help clean up, Mrs. Froede," Penny said as she got up quickly.

"Not now, Penny—thanks anyway. Paul's in a hurry, so you run along. These dishes won't take me any time." She shooed Penny out of the kitchen.

Ten minutes later they were threading their way through the traffic of the giant city. Penny rode in front with Froede, while Mark and David sat in the back.

"We're heading for the Egyptian Antiquities Museum," Froede exclaimed, swerving sharply to avoid a cab that had lunged in front of them. "The place is fantastic! You won't be able to take it all in, so don't try—we'll just see a few of the rooms today. Then, when you've been in Egypt for a while, we'll come back and look again. There's just too much to see in one visit."

Finally they turned off the broad boulevard onto a narrow street. Froede continued to tell them about the museum. "A century and a half ago, Egypt was being robbed of its ancient treasures. Foreigners were stealing the stuff in boatloads! And Egyptian leaders were giving priceless old things away to foreign princes and dignitaries! It was plunder, pure and simple!

"Eventually, a French scholar by the name of Champollion demanded that the Egyptian government stop this looting! That was in 1830. Five years later, a commission was formed—the Service des Antiquities de l'Egypt—and this group began gathering the finds from tombs and tombs and storing them in Cairo. The stealing by foreigners was stopped. It was a great start.

"But trust politicians to be politicians! Just twenty years later, the Egyptian Pasha gave the whole collection to the Austrian Archduke when he visited Egypt!" Froede shook his head in disgust.

"That's when another hero arose—Auguste Mariette. Every schoolchild in the world should know that man's name! He was also French, and a top-notch archaeologist. He got the support of the famous Ferdinand de Lesseps, and together they persuaded the Pasha to appoint him as the Director of Antiquities."

Froede looked quickly at Penny. "Young lady, you're a student of French. Who was Ferdinand de Lesseps?"

"He designed the Suez Canal," she replied without hesitation, smiling at this vigorous man who kept them all on their toes.

"You bet he did! The man was a genius. The Egyptians were really in his debt for that canal, so they took his advice and put Mariette in charge of all their antiquities. That meant all their ancient tombs, tombs, ruins, statues—you name it, Mariette was in charge of it. Once again, the robbery of Egypt's treasures stopped. By this time, some dedicated Egyptians were behind him.

"It all goes to show you what one person can do!" He paused, thought a moment, then spoke emphatically. "You young folks remember that. Your lives can count for something—if you want them to!"

Froede turned the car again and pulled into a parking lot across from a stately classical building.

"Follow me," he said as they got out. Together they walked from the car to the building that housed so many treasures from Egypt's magnificent past. "I'm going to park you three in one of the rooms while I make a quick visit to the director. He's expecting me. Then I'll rejoin you. Keep your eyes open—I don't have to tell you that! And don't talk of the matters we discussed last night. Not with anyone. Not anywhere." He frowned at David and Mark, but softened the threatening effect by winking at Penny.

Froede led them into the entrance, then turned left and took them down a hall until they came to the beard of the Great Sphinx. Here they stopped and stood, feasting their eyes on the ancient carving. "You've probably seen pictures of this," Froede said.

Then he rushed them back toward the entrance, but suddenly turned left into a room with ancient boats along each side. "These are funerary boats," Froede explained, waving his arms to left and right. "They were buried with Senworset the Third. Look at the small boards—they didn't have long timbers to work with—and see how they put those pieces together. The boats are a marvel of craftsmanship!"

He looked at his watch. "I'll leave you here. Mark, take this map of the museum. We're in this room." He pointed to Hall 43. "Stick around this area—Halls 43, 48, and 47. I'll be back in half an hour." He hurried out of the room and down the corridor.

Time seemed to stand still as the three wandered before the statues in the halls. There were not many visitors in the rooms, and soon they felt lost in history, transported back through centuries, as they marveled at the craftsmanship of workers who had been dead for several thousand years. Neither Mark, Penny, nor David had ever experienced history in such a way.

Mark wandered off to ponder the collection of knives made of flint and obsidian. Penny and David strolled, entranced, along the rows of treasures, stopping finally before the statue of a curiously hunched figure. They read the sign and learned that the statue was of Hetepdief, a priest of the early Egyptian dynasties. The sign also said that the inscriptions on his shoulder gave his titles as well as the name of his father.

Penny and David felt as if they were suddenly in the presence of the man himself. She looked up at David as he gazed at the statue of the ancient priest. David smiled at her and seemed to read her thoughts. "This is incredible!" he said wonderingly. "I feel like we're back in time with that man! Everything seems so peaceful and—and so incredibly old."

Penny smiled back, overcome suddenly with the thought that if they just closed their eyes and made a wish, they'd wake up in ancient Egypt and speak with the priest himself! She wondered if David were thinking the same thing. Neither of them wanted the moment to end.

Something moved into the corner of Penny's vision; she turned her head to look—and froze!

"David," she whispered, clutching his arm, "there's Hoffmann!"

CHAPTER 4

HOFFMANN!

David spun around, looked toward the door, and took a deep breath. She was right! The trim blond man in a tan suit was striding down the hall to their left, looking straight ahead as he passed the entrance of the room in which they stood.

"Get back!" David pulled Penny quickly behind a thick column.

Hoffmann passed from view. He hadn't glanced their way.

"That's him all right!" David said. "The ringleader of the gang that chased us down the river! Colonel Lamumba told your father that he got away."

The peaceful atmosphere of the museum was shattered. Suddenly, Penny felt the same fear she'd known on the river just four days before, when they'd paddled their canoe desperately to escape the men pursuing them. And Hoffmann had been their leader!

"What's he doing *here*?" she asked in an anguished whisper.

"I don't know!" David replied. "How could he have reached Cairo so *fast*?" Then he had a sudden thought. "He didn't look at us, but could he see Mark?"

They looked to their right. Mark was down that hall, but not in sight.

"Good," David said gratefully. "Hoffmann couldn't see him either. Let's go find him."

They moved quickly down the hall, turned into the next door, and found Mark studying a case of ancient knives.

The sturdy, blond boy looked up as they approached. He grinned and was about to tell them about the knives when he noticed their solemn faces.

"What's wrong?" he asked quickly.

"We just saw Hoffmann go down the hall," Penny exclaimed, pointing back. "He didn't see us."

"Hoffmann! *Here*?" Mark asked. "How did he get here as fast as we did?"

"Colonel Lamumba said he'd escaped with one of his men. Do you think he's here because of your father's project with Mr. Froede?" David added.

"How could he know about *that*?" Mark asked wondering.

"Remember the spy in your father's office—Mr. Sanderson—the man who ran away?" David asked. "Couldn't he have learned something of your father's work with Mr. Froede? Maybe he suspected a big deal going on—he'd be sure to tell the people he worked for. And that includes Hoffmann!" David turned back to watch the entrance.

"I think you're right, David," Penny said. Her dark eyes were deeply troubled. "We'd be fools to think he didn't know of Dad's work with Mr. Froede in Egypt. Mr. Sanderson's been with Dad for years. He's bound to have picked up something."

"You've got to be right, both of you," Mark agreed. "Dad and Mr. Froede didn't talk about this project in the office—Mr. Froede told us that—but Sanderson had to know Dad and Mr. Froede were planning something." Mark's open face showed his anxiety.

"We can't let Hoffmann see us," David said. "Let's wait here for Mr. Froede and keep an eye on the door. He said he'd find us in one of these rooms. If Hoffmann comes back, we'll duck behind this boat."

The spell cast by the ancient treasures and statues was gone. For the next ten minutes the three stood anxiously huddled together, talking in low tones as they waited for Mr. Froede.

He surprised them by coming through a small door in the wall behind the boat. They jumped when he spoke. "Hi! What do you think of these treasures?"

The smile faded from his face when he saw their expressions. "What's wrong?" he asked.

"We just saw Hoffmann go by," Penny said quickly. "Dad told you about him—the man in charge of the gang that chased us on the river. He was trying to steal the diamond mine Dad's people found."

"Hoffmann!" Froede's voice was sharp. "Here? I can't believe it." He glanced quickly around. "Where did he go?"

David told him and added, "He was moving fast and

didn't look this way. We don't think he saw us."

Froede acted instantly. "Come with me!" He took Penny's arm and led them quickly to the small door from which he'd come. They entered a narrow hall and moved rapidly to a door on their right. Opening that, he led them into a large and elegantly furnished room.

"Wait here!" he commanded as he left them and went through another door. The three looked around at the richly furnished office with its marble floor covered by a deep maroon carpet. Two life-sized tan stone statues of men with crocodile heads flanked the door through which Froede had disappeared. To the left of the door stood a long glass case with golden jewelry spread on dark velvet and gleaming in the light from the tall window beside it.

"Look at those necklaces!" Penny exclaimed, moving over to the case.

But the boys were studying the crocodile-headed statues. "What evil faces!" David said, looking at the weird creatures. "It's not right—mixing beasts and men like that!"

In a few minutes Froede appeared, a pleased expression on his face. "Let's go!" He led them out the door through which he'd just come and down another, wider hall. Before they knew it, they were outside, squinting in the bright sunlight.

"We're going home," Froede explained, setting a fast pace though the parked cars. "I'll show you the museum another time."

Utterly mystified at the turn of events, they followed him to the car. Froede drove out of the parking lot and into the busy city traffic. As he drove, he began to explain.

"I went to the director," he said. "He let me use his private phone to call my government contact. I told him about Hoffmann—I know more about that man than you kids do—and he assured me they would capture him. There's a security team assigned to protect our work, and they're closing in on the museum now."

"But how could Hoffmann get to Cairo so soon?" Penny asked anxiously. "He got here as fast as we did!"

"And why is he here in the first place?" Mark asked. "Does he know something about your work with Dad?"

"Yes, he does," Froede said. "That spy in your Dad's office must have tipped off Hoffmann's gang about all your father's communications with me. Your Dad and I send each other fax messages regularly and sometimes talk by phone. But we've never said a word about this tomb except face to face."

He swerved the car to avoid a man on a bike, then continued. "But Sanderson's job would have been to gather any information he could about all the communications from our firm, so he must have suspected that we have something important going on here." He set his face grimly at the thought of the man's betrayal. "And he passed that information on to the people who were paying him."

He drove skillfully through the traffic as the young

folks digested this information. "But how he got to Cairo so fast is a mystery to me. He's got to have powerful connections."

"What does this mean, Uncle Paul?" Penny asked. "Will it stop your project?"

"Not on your life, young lady!" Froede smiled emphatically. "The police will pick up Hoffmann—they want him in Africa. He's out of the picture! And we'll get right to work. We'll leave this afternoon, in fact. There's no sense waiting another day."

He glanced quickly at Penny. "We've nipped this in the bud. If you hadn't spotted Hoffmann, he might have done us some real damage. What a break this is!"

He began to whistle a cheerful tune, and soon Mark, Penny, and David relaxed.

David thought of the shock he'd felt when he saw Hoffmann. But the police would get him! The justice he'd escaped in Africa would catch him now!

Back in the Egyptian Antiquities Museum, a trim blond man whose body seemed to contain more power than his size suggested approached a desk in an inner office. With precise, controlled motions he took out a business card and presented it to the secretary. She read the name, rose at once, and led him without knocking into the office of an aide to the director.

In less than a minute the blond man emerged with the aide, a large corpulent man in a dark suit. The aide snapped to his secretary as he passed, "I'll be gone for an hour. Hold any messages until I return. If the director asks for me, tell him an emergency arose. I'll explain when I get back."

"Yes, Mr. Salin," the woman replied.

Both men moved quickly into the hall, turned left, and disappeared into the passageway leading to the director's private parking place.

CHAPTER 5

INTO THE TOMB

Froede pulled into his driveway, jumped out, and hurried into the house. "Pack your things—we leave in an hour," he said over his shoulder as he dashed inside.

And leave in an hour they did! Penny felt they hardly had time to thank Mrs. Froede for her hospitality, and she felt worse that they hadn't spent more time with her.

"Nonsense, Penny," Mrs. Froede laughed. "Paul didn't bring you here to spend time with me. He needs you to do translation and photography for him! You know how glad I am when you visit, so plan on more leisure time when you get back from the desert. I want to take you shopping."

She hugged the three of them as her husband put their luggage in the car. He kissed her, jumped in, backed out the drive, and headed for a private airfield on the outskirts of the giant city.

"We'll fly to the project in the company's helicopter," he told them as he drove. "By the way, we'll use the word 'project' for what we're doing—never mention *tomb*!" The kids agreed quickly, intrigued by the deepening mystery of this adventure.

Almost an hour later they'd passed the city limits.

31

Not long after that, Froede turned into a drive blocked by a gate. A tall wire fence stretched to the left and right enclosing a private airfield. David saw a guard emerge from a shack behind the gate and walk toward them. The man recognized Froede, opened the gate, and waved them in.

David counted three small buildings and a hangar as they drove in. A helicopter was parked in front of the hangar with two men standing beside it. To the left, two cars and a small truck were neatly parked. To the right, a tall radio tower soared into the clear blue sky. As they drove closer and parked, David could see a satellite dish surrounded by its own wire fence.

Froede jumped out, followed by Mark, Penny, and David. Quickly he introduced them to two men. "Mr. Chastain and Mr. Rierra—our pilots," he explained. They all shook hands.

David was impressed by the men. Rierra was stocky, black-haired, and powerfully built. Chastain was just as muscular but was taller than Rierra by six inches. Both were friendly; yet David felt the controlled strength in their handshakes. He suspected that they were fighting men as well as pilots. *This company must be involved in a lot of interesting work!* he thought

Froede gave them no time for speculation. "Let's put our gear in the helicopter," he called as he walked around the car and unlocked the trunk. The youngsters followed him, retrieving their packs along with several other bags Froede had brought. Rierra and Chastain helped them carry their gear to the helicopter.

"The other stuff's already aboard," Rierra told Froede, "and your instruments."

"Fine. Where's Ed?"

"In the office, clearing our flight with traffic control," Chastain replied. "He's got us heading west first. Then we change course and fly to the project from there. He's plotted an indirect approach—in case anyone's tracking us on radar."

"Excellent!" Froede nodded his approval. David noticed his unceasing vigilance; he was darting quick glances in every direction.

"Do you want one of us to stay with you on the site?" Rierra asked.

"Not yet," Froede answered. "Give us a day or two. By that time, Keno should have a clear idea of where we want to go. Then I'll give you a call."

He squinted up at the sky. It was perfectly clear. "When will Foucachon and André arrive?"

"Day after tomorrow," Chastain said. "They'll be ready to back you up whenever you say."

"Very good!" Froede was pleased with these arrangements—and with the team that would support them. He turned to Mark, Penny, and David.

"Foucachon and André are—how shall I put it?— very versatile and useful men! They'll join us when we want more help guarding the information we'll get from Keno's translations. Until then, we're keeping a

low profile as if nothing important's going on." He
smacked his fist into his palm with great satisfaction
and strode rapidly toward the office. "I'll be right
back." Chastain followed him.

"I don't suppose you three have been in a helicopter," Rierra said. "Let me show you around." He
headed toward the waiting machine whose long blades
dropped almost to the ground.

David, Penny, and Mark exchanged grins as they
trooped after him. Penny almost laughed, but Mark put
his finger quickly to his lips. "Never been in a helicopter!" *Oh, yeah*! she thought. Just four days before
they'd run for a roaring camouflaged military machine
with a canoe strapped to its skids and rocketed into the
sky, barely escaping a gang of wild pigs!

But they said nothing of this to Rierra as they followed him dutifully into the helicopter. And, indeed,
this craft was nothing like the army chopper they'd
travelled in four days ago. Painted a gleaming white,
trimmed with red and blue, luxuriously furnished
inside—this was more like the Gulfstream IV corporate jet they'd flown in than the sparse army helicopter
with bucket seats that had lifted them out of the jungle.

Rierra was showing them the cockpit when Froede
spoke suddenly behind them. "Let's be off!"

Then everything seemed to happen at once. Rierra
directed Penny and David to two seats by a window on
the left side of the craft; Froede and Mark sat together
on the right. They all buckled their seatbelts as the

pilots went forward. Soon the engines began to whine. Then they felt the machine begin to vibrate with the movement of the giant rotors.

Froede leaned over and spoke to Penny above the increasing noise. "They're going to circle the Pyramids and the Sphinx so you can take some pictures. Get your camera ready."

Penny gasped with glad surprise and began to rummage in her camera case. The Pyramids! Pictures of a lifetime!

As Penny worked with her camera, David looked across at Mark and grinned. What an adventure!

The roar of the engines increased, the machine began to shudder, and they were in the air, circling.

The helicopter sped across the great desert, heading first to the west, before turning south, then east—to the hidden tomb!

CHAPTER 6

THE SEALED TREASURE

Back in Cairo, a royal blue Mercedes pulled out of the private parking place of the director of the Egyptian Antiquities Museum and entered the busy stream of traffic. In the luxurious, grey upholstered backseat of the car, Hoffmann sat erect and fumed silently. Why had this fat slob rushed him out of the office?

The secretary had no sooner ushered him in, when this arrogant man had rushed from behind his desk and commanded, "Come with me!" Now, as the Mercedes sped along the wide boulevard, Hoffmann determined to discover the meaning of their sudden exodus from the museum.

Slouched to Hoffmann's left, the corpulent Mr. Salin flicked a gold cigarette case out of his coat pocket, extracted a long slender cigarette, placed it carefully in an ivory holder, and positioned the holder delicately between his thick lips.

Hoffmann, lean and fit, eyed the large flabby man with barely concealed contempt. "Where are we

36

going?" he asked curtly.

The large, soft Egyptian inhaled deeply and blew smoke toward the glass window that separated them from the chauffeur in front. He frowned accusingly at the German beside him.

"You were recognized as soon as you entered the museum."

Hoffmann's jaw dropped! "Who could have known me there? I only arrived this morning!"

"I don't know. All I know is that my secretary signalled me to activate the listening device tuned to the director's office. When I did, a voice I didn't recognize was already talking on the phone, asking for someone on the security team. When he got his man, he told him you were in the museum and should be picked up at once."

Salin frowned at Hoffmann over his long cigarette. "Then he said to whomever he was talking to, 'We'll go to the site right away,' and he hung up."

The Egyptian inhaled deeply and continued, "I dialed the emergency number at once and said I was bringing my visitor to the restaurant earlier than I'd planned. That's what I was told to do if anything strange occurred."

Suddenly Salin leaned to his left and glanced into the rearview window. He wanted to see if they were being followed. Apparently satisfied, he sat back, slouching, and looked at Hoffmann.

He continued, "Early this morning I received a call from Schmidt telling me that you were coming. I was told to brief you on your assignment." He reached into his bulging coat pocket and handed Hoffmann a thick envelope. "These are your orders! I couldn't explain them to you at the museum as I'd planned because the police were on their way to pick you up."

The Egyptian paused. Hoffmann still hadn't thanked him for the lightning escape. "I got you out of there just in time!" Salin barked. Still Hoffmann expressed no appreciation for the deftness with which he'd been delivered from certain arrest. *These ungrateful bullies!* Salin thought, shaking his heavy head in disgust.

But he had received his orders, and he proceeded to carry them out. "You've been told about the tomb Daring's and Froede's firm has found under the sand. There's a fortune buried there in treasure rooms that have never been opened. That treasure will be found by Paul Froede and his team. When they find it, our people will dispose of Froede's crew and then hold him and his translator for you to question."

Hoffmann's face showed no emotion. This kind of operation was not new to him.

Salin continued, "This afternoon, you will be flown to a small oasis that is just sixty kilometers from the buried tomb. Four men are waiting for you there. They will be under your command. You'll wait there until we signal you that Froede has found the treasure. Then you will drive at once to the site."

Salin glanced back again to see if their car was being followed. Although the air-conditioned luxury sedan was quite cool, Salin was sweating. Hoffmann smiled contemptuously at the Egyptian's fears.

Salin continued his briefing. "We have men in Froede's crew—his foreman, Ahmet, and two others. They will radio us when Froede has found the treasure. You will question Froede and his translator. We know there is a way out from the treasure rooms to the Nile River. You must make them tell you where it is. That will not take long! Then close them in with the others to suffocate. When they are dead—Ahmet will know— your men and his will enter the tomb and follow the secret passage to the Nile."

Salin looked nervously ahead. "It's time for us to drop you off. I must hurry. That tunnel from the river was made when the tomb itself was built to enable them to bring the treasure, the coffins—everything— into the tomb. It was far easier to move such things by boat than across the desert."

Again he blew smoke toward the glass partition. "You will proceed down that tunnel to the river, open that entrance from the inside, and let in our men. Until you do that, they have no way of finding the river entrance to the tomb. They will come by night, wait in their boats in the general area they expect you to exit, and watch for your signal. You will lead them back to the treasure rooms and help them remove all the treasure they can carry through the tunnel. Put all this on the boat. The plan is simplicity itself." He smiled faintly.

"That treasure will bring us a fortune on the black markets of the world. We'll be able to continue financing all our espionage activities—in spite of the KGB's slashed budget!"

He looked sternly at Hoffmann. "Don't let anything—or anyone—stand in your way. You must get that treasure!"

Hoffmann was stunned by the uncertain aspects of the plan. "What if I can't get Froede and his man to talk?"

"You may not have to. Our men in Paris are busy deciphering an ancient hieroglyphic stone that has a map of part of the tomb. That stone was broken off from a larger stone in the museum here in Cairo, and together they give complete directions for reaching the treasure rooms and the river. It's amazing that we found out about it—but that's another story.

"When the people in Paris have deciphered the directions to the tunnel they will fax that information to Ahmet. He will lead you to it. They are very close now to deciphering the hieroglyphics." The Egyptian glanced at Hoffmann with a crooked smile. "Besides, I'm sure you will be able to force from Froede and his man the information that they have gained."

The sedan decreased speed and Salin looked up quickly. "There's the car that will take you to the plane. Study the directions I gave you. I'll call you as soon as we learn that Froede has found the treasure."

The Mercedes stopped suddenly behind a parked

green Volvo. Hoffmann stepped quickly out and into the car whose back door opened to receive him. The Mercedes pulled back into the street, gained momentum, and sped down the boulevard. The Volvo waited a minute, then followed the Mercedes for a block before turning sharply to the right down a narrow street.

CHAPTER 7

THE SECRETS IN HIEROGLYPHICS

Rising early as usual, David and Mark went outside into the cool morning air and began to exercise. This was their fourth day in Egypt—the third at the tomb site—and they were beginning to feel they were back in shape.

"In shape! In shape!" Penny had teased them the day before. "All you boys think about is staying in shape. You're just physical fitness freaks, that's all." She hit Mark's flat stomach. "Look at that fat! You've got a long way to go, Mark!" Her eyes laughed at David.

Her jibes were all in jest, however. She did exercises every day also, but not with the boys.

As Mark and David ran in place beside the mobile home in which they lived, they talked about the events of the past three days.

The helicopter had brought them down to this desolate spot in the desert, surrounded by undulating sand dunes which stretched away in the distance like waves in the ocean. The desert emptiness was broken only by the five large mobile homes, a large pickup truck, and two vans. A cluster of fuel drums stood near the power unit that supplied the mobile homes, and another cluster of barrels contained fresh water.

Exiting the helicopter, Froede had led the three of them to the largest mobile home. "You folks will live here with me. We've got a private room for Penny, beds for the rest of us, kitchen, and bath with a shower. It's a luxury! The men live in those two trailers over there. That one with the radio antenna is our office and the one behind it is our lab. Believe it or not, there's a lot of room in these things!"

He led them into a surprisingly spacious interior, tastefully decorated with green curtains and rugs, and showed Penny her room at the back. After they had put away their gear, he took them to the office to meet Keno and Ahmet.

Keno was slender, white-haired, and solemn with deep-set eyes in his lined face. Ahmet was tall and darker than his companion; he beamed with pleasure at meeting them. An exceedingly friendly man, he gripped their hands with great enthusiasm and offered to show them around the camp.

"Thank you, Ahmet," Froede said gratefully. "I'll study the messages while you do that. Looks like a ton of information came in while I was gone." With a frown of concentration knitting his brow, he began to rummage through the fax messages on his desk. Keno remained with him.

Later, after eating supper in the mobile home, Penny, Mark, and David sat outside with Froede, identifying the constellations that shone so brilliantly in the clear desert sky. Because Cairo was far north from where Mark and Penny lived, they saw stars they hadn't seen for a long time.

The kids were dying to see the tomb—the "project" as they called it—but they'd arrived too late to see it that day. "We'll go in the morning," Froede said. "Let me tell you one of our rules, however. We never go into the project without taking a pack—each of us. That's something I learned a long time ago."

"What's in the pack?" Mark asked. It sounded like the packs his dad had him carry in the bush.

"A canteen with fresh water, a couple of flashlights, some light sticks that burn for an hour when broken, a knife, some food, a compass—survival gear, in other words. That way, if you're cut off or trapped or lost, you'll have something to keep you going until we get you out. Not that we expect anything like that to happen! But we just go prepared—always. There's a pack ready for each of you."

Froede got up. "Let's turn in. We've got a big day ahead. Tomorrow morning, you three will see the sights of your lives!"

And see the sights of their lives they did! After exercise, Bible study, and breakfast, they followed Froede, Ahmet, and Keno to the large tunnel entrance. It sloped deep into the ground to the tomb door below. Steps had been cut at a steep angle in the close-packed sand and the party descended until they reached the bottom. There they faced a seven-foot-high stone door.

"Give us a hand, boys," Froede said, as he and Ahmet felt for the grooves that had been cut in the door. Mark and David joined them and helped the two men lift the massive stone outward and open, laying it back carefully against the wall to which it was hinged.

"There are counterweights inside, to help us move this thing," Froede told them. "Otherwise, it would take a dozen men."

They entered the hall of the tomb, breathless with excitement. Froede and the two Egyptians led, while Mark, Penny, and David followed, their hearts pounding. Froede and Keno carried battery-powered lamps to light their way.

Their eyes were wide with amazement as they looked at the walls decorated with larger-than-life figures: ranks of marching soldiers, crowds of servants, weirdly dressed priests, huge figures of men with crocodile heads, cobras, curious-looking dogs, and cattle. David thought that the eyes of the crocodile-headed men followed him wherever he walked. He mentioned it to Mark and Penny, and they agreed at once. The walls told history, the history of people who lived and died four thousand years ago!

Penny shuddered, and when David looked at her, she smiled weakly. "I just felt a chill all of a sudden. It's gone now." She laughed nervously, but he knew exactly what she was feeling. There was evil on the faces of the crocodile heads. They all realized that it wasn't just ancient art they were seeing. Those paintings were also the expression of occult religion!

They walked down the long entrance hall of the tomb, following the light of their flashlights and feeling small in the tiny area of light that moved through the overarching darkness of the place. To their right, Froede said, was a smaller room that they had found just a week ago. David saw the open doorway, but darkness covered whatever was within.

When they reached the far wall, they set down their packs. "We'll leave you with Keno for a while," Froede said. "He'll show you what we've found so far. He'll keep you busy too! Ahmet and I have work to do outside." He waved and followed Ahmet back to the entrance of the tunnel.

Keno asked the three to help him set up his equipment. The solemn Egyptian positioned battery-powered lamps so they would illuminate the hieroglyphics that he wanted to translate. He had the boys hold the lamps while he studied the wall, and then motioned them to move the lights to one side or another for the clearest view of the ancient symbols he had to translate.

David was struck by the long shadows cast on the wall when one of them moved in front of the lamps. He felt as though they were in a small patch of light surrounded by a sea of ominous, spirit-infested darkness. There was a heaviness to the air which reminded him of the immeasurable weight of the tomb above them—and of the many feet of sand above that!

When Keno was satisfied with the position of the lamps, he began to study the hieroglyphics, consulting a thick notebook as he did so. Then slowly he began to translate the strange symbols into English, speaking into a microcassette recorder.

His translation proceeded slowly. Often he stopped to look up a word; sometimes he stopped to erase what he'd spoken and make a new translation. When he was satisfied with the words he'd chosen, he gave the boys the signal to translate into the microcassettes they also carried. It was very exacting work—which surprised both Mark and David, who'd thought that this would be a rather easy task!

Keno showed Penny which sections of the wall to photograph. "We'll have the pictures and my translations as well," he said. "With more time and information, a better translation can be made later."

Mark dictated a French translation of Keno's words into his recorder; David did the same in German. The boys stayed very alert, trying to express Keno's English accurately in the foreign languages they'd studied for years.

The story Keno read from the hieroglyphics was fascinating, telling of the pharaoh's wars, victory parades, and, finally, his building of the tomb. A marvelous history of ancient culture unfolded before them. They began to feel a part of this long-ago people who had been just as real in their time as Mark, Penny, and David were now!

On their second day there, Keno reached the section describing the layout of the tomb itself with directions for opening the doors to the passages and rooms beyond.

"Mr. Froede and I have not let the others see this panel," he explained softly, as he showed Penny exactly what part of the wall he wanted photographed. "This is the key to the whole inner part of the tomb. Only you three, and Mr. Froede and I will know about this. Let me have your tapes as soon as you finish them, and I'll give them to Mr. Froede. As well as your film, Penny."

He looked at them with growing excitement in his dark solemn eyes. "This is an unbelievable discovery and there is a treasure beyond imagination in the tomb itself. When we enter that tomb, you three will behold wonders few people on earth have ever seen! And, Penny, Mr. Froede has received permission for you to photograph that treasure, once the government officials have arrived. That is a great honor." He smiled at the ecstatic girl.

They took a break for lunch, coming up into the glaring sun that struck from above as well as by reflection from the pure white sand around them. Because of the brightness, they ate lunch inside their mobile home with Froede and Keno. The Egyptians took naps after lunch, Froede studied his papers and maps, and the youngsters read and talked about the things Keno had translated.

After their rest, they went back to the tomb and

worked until late afternoon. When they'd finished eating dinner, Froede and Keno developed Penny's pictures while she typed into her laptop computer the dictation the Egyptian had given as he translated. When the three had finished their work, they went out to study the bright stars through Froede's binoculars. This had quickly become their routine. Never far from the camp, they were lost in wonder in the vast universe of desert sky.

As they were exercising on this, their third day in the desert, Mark and David discussed what had happened. When they were thoroughly warmed up, they sparred vigorously against each other for half an hour. Then they cooled down with lighter exercises and went inside the mobile home to shower.

After dressing in khaki shorts and shirts, they sat outside under the awning in the cool morning air and studied their Bibles until Penny called them inside to breakfast. They joined her and Mr. Froede around the small table. Penny also wore khaki pants, and a khaki headband held back her hair. David wished he could take a picture of her right then.

The men ate the fruit, bread, and eggs she'd fixed for them in vast amounts.

"We just want you to know we appreciate what you do for us, Penny," David said, reaching for more eggs.

"That's right," Mark added, taking more bread. "We know how easily girls get their feelings hurt. Dad said we just couldn't let that happen in Egypt so I promised him we'd do our best to keep you happy. We can't have you coming unglued. Is that all the bread?"

Her bright eyes sparkled as she got up to bring them more food. "You two must be the kindest, most thoughtful guys in the whole world! Think of all the girls who never get to meet boys so kind and considerate—and hungry!"

Froede laughed. "That's right, Penny. Compliment them. Keep feeding them too. I need strong workers."

When they finished, Froede got up, stepped outside for a minute, then returned and sat down. Something in his manner caught their attention. His mood had changed. He seemed to hesitate; then he spoke, choosing his words with care.

"While you were exercising, I received a message on my fax over there." He gestured to the desk against the wall. "It was from our security team in Cairo."

He hesitated again. "It said that Hoffmann escaped the museum before he could be picked up and that he'd vanished. They warned me to be on guard. Two of our men will join us tomorrow to beef up our security." He frowned at them for a moment. "I don't know why they didn't tell me this three days ago. Maybe they thought they'd pick him up."

This was sobering news. Penny spoke first, her brown eyes troubled. "Do you think he would be after anything on this project, Uncle Paul?"

"I don't know, Penny. We know they're looking for

money anyplace they can find it." Froede replied. He paused, furrows wrinkling his tanned brow. "Yet it sure is something of a coincidence that Hoffmann would be in the museum in Cairo, just when your dad's firm and mine are involved in this work. And just after he failed to rob your dad of the mining rights in Africa. He's clearly after big money—and that's what we're on top of right now!"

He slapped his leg with the palm of his hand and stood up. "But we've got nothing to worry about. I promised your mom you'd be safe with me, and I've no reason to change my mind. Our men here are alert. And this is really a project for the Egyptian government. Nothing could be safer than that." He began putting together the pack he always took to the tomb.

"Still," he added, "just be alert for anything unusual, and tell me at once if you see anything strange—anything at all." He looked carefully at each of them in turn to emphasize these words.

"Time to go to work," he said briskly, breaking the somber mood. "Bring your packs." As they rushed to get ready, David saw Froede swiftly slip a small automatic out of his desk drawer and into his trouser pocket. David looked quickly away, and Froede didn't notice that he had seen the gun.

The three followed Froede out into the sunlight to the steps that led down to the tomb. Keno and Ahmet were waiting for them. All of them descended the steep steps, opened the heavy door, and began the day's work.

CHAPTER 8

TRAPPED!

The tension was terrific! Keno was translating at a rapid rate, as fast as he could read, David thought, pouring out words which described the way to the inner tomb and its treasures. Penny held the recorder to his face while Mark and David labored to keep up with their translations of Keno's English. The three felt as if they were following a running tour guide to the price-less wealth of the pharaoh's chamber!

They were studying the right-hand wall of the room. Their two lamps were placed on the floor, casting bright light on the paintings and the hieroglyphics that were unlocking the four-thousand-year-old secrets of the tomb.

An hour before, Keno had stopped, his eyes shining, and told them he needed to speak to Froede for a minute. He went down the long hall and up the steep steps, returning a quarter of an hour later. The kids decided that he'd gone to brief Froede on what he'd learned, but they didn't ask and he didn't volunteer any information. He was clearly very excited and pleased.

They had gone back to work and been busy for another two hours, when Froede suddenly came up behind them. "Keno, I need to borrow David for a few minutes."

"Certainly," Keno replied, stepping back from the wall whose signs he'd been reading so intently.

He turned and looked at Froede. "I've found the key, Paul!" His solemn face broke into a slow smile. "We know about all the vital rooms now." Excitement shook his quiet voice. "But I've been rushing—and haste does not make for accuracy—not when you're translating, and certainly not when you're translating ancient hieroglyphics! It will be good for me to rest a few minutes."

He sighed and turned away from the wall and its secret lore—coded lore that he with his knowledge was unlocking by the minute. Penny and Mark looked quizzically at Froede and David as they walked away.

David followed Froede down the hall. Before they reached the entrance, however, Froede turned left and led him through a narrow door and into the blackness of a small side room. Their way was illuminated only by the light in Froede's hand. David and his friends had never entered this room before, and he was filled with a strange foreboding.

Froede strode quickly to the far wall of the room and turned his large flashlight beam in a slow arc to show David the dramatic scene. The wall was decorated with a huge painting of a titanic battle between life-sized fighting men. The colors were brilliant; the fighting men seemed to come alive as Froede directed his light over them.

The pharaoh, standing in a war chariot, was leading his army to victory over invading soldiers. Men were fallen and crushed between the chariot wheels of the Egyptians in a dramatic fresco which covered the entire side of the room. Units of soldiers with spears held erect marched behind the pharaoh. Before them the enemy fled in panic.

"Quick, David," Froede said urgently, breaking into David's thoughts. "Give me a hand!" He bent and began to press the wall at the hub of the pharaoh's chariot wheel. "Push here," he said.

David knelt, placed his right hand next to Froede's, and pressed against the stone. To David's astonishment, a whole section of the wall began to move, swinging on an invisible hinge, opening onto a dark void beyond.

"That's enough," Froede said. "Now push this side and close it."

David pushed against the stone block until the wall was flush again. There was so sign of the door they had opened! David looked closely; the lines of the chariot spokes and raised spears of standing soldiers were painted so cleverly that the cracks could not be seen.

"There's no time to explain, David!" Froede said earnestly. "Just look at this chariot wheel. Could you find it again?"

David studied the spot Froede indicated, the place they had pushed, noting its relation to the other wall.

"Yes, sir!" he replied. "It's the last chariot before the

corner where these two walls join. I can find it." His heart was thudding—not just because of the mysterious opening, but also because of Froede's solemn manner.

Froede jumped up. "Let's start back before anyone comes. That's the entrance to the tunnel that leads to the treasure room, as well as to the river beyond. Only you and Keno know this—so far. That tunnel ends in the caves that front the river, and that's why it has air. Through all the centuries, some of those caves have remained intact."

He led David back to the door, then paused, looking carefully into the large entrance hall which was lit by a column of sunlight flooding down from the tunnel above. He turned to face David then; his brow was furrowed, his eyes deeply troubled.

"David, if something happens to me and we're separated, lead Penny and Mark through that tunnel to the river. About forty yards from the entrance we opened, you'll find another battle scene painted on the right-hand wall. There should be another picture with the same kind of chariot wheel as the one on the wall we just opened. I haven't been there yet, but Keno's read about it from the hieroglyphics. That's the entrance to the treasure room, but you won't need to go in there. Just follow the tunnel to the river and make your escape."

Then Froede paused and looked soberly at David. "If for some reason you can't get out the tunnel exit to the river, go back to the treasure room. Press the chariot wheel and go in. On the other side of the room you'll

find a third picture of pharaoh's chariot. It opens the
wall just like this one does and leads to a different exit
to the river. The two tunnels come out near each other.
That's all Keno's been able to learn so far."

He took a deep breath. His blue eyes were troubled.
"I underestimated the danger from Hoffmann and his
accomplices. But if anything happens, I'll try to head
them off so you three can get away. Now go back to
work and act normally. We may pull this off yet."

David was completely mystified. He wanted to ask
questions, but Froede gave him no chance. The well-
muscled man grinned his jaunty grin, hit David's
shoulder with his powerful hand, and strode confidently toward the door. David followed.

Suddenly they heard the sound of footsteps rushing
down the steep steps from the entrance above ground.
Froede pushed David down the hall. "Get back to the
others. Keep working. Say nothing of this if you don't
have to. I'll try to head things off." Froede turned left
to meet the descending man; David turned right and
walked quickly to rejoin Mark and Penny.

A man's legs came into view on the steep steps from
the desert floor above them. It was Ahmet. David
could hear the Egyptian's question.

"Mr. Froede," Ahmet said, as he reached the floor of
the tomb hall, "can you come outside? My men tell me
we have a problem with the power system."

"Certainly, Ahmet," Froede replied. He raced up the
steep stairs with Ahmet struggling to keep up.

Just as David reached the wall where Keno, Mark, and Penny were waiting, Froede's voice echoed down the tunnel. "Keno, can you join us for a minute? Ahmet says we may need your help."

"Right away, Paul," Keno called back. He turned to Mark, Penny, and David with his gracious smile. "I don't think I'll be long." Then he walked toward the entrance and up the stairs to the outside.

Keno joined Froede and Ahmet in the bright sunlight above the buried tomb and began to follow them to the power plant. As he did so, he happened to glance back at the entrance from which he'd just come. What he saw caused him to stop in surprise!

Ahmet's two men, with another worker Keno hadn't seen before had moved swiftly to the tunnel entrance and begun to descend the steep stairs to the stone door below. Keno opened his mouth to ask what they were up to, but before he could speak Ahmet pulled a revolver from under his shirt and pointed it at Froede and Keno. The foreman's friendly smile was gone; now his face was set in a decisive mask.

"Mr. Froede, I'll ask you and Keno to go to the trailer. At once!"

Keno was astounded. Froede only pretended to be. This was what he'd feared.

"What in the world are you doing with that pistol?" Froede asked indignantly, playing the game. His mind was racing. *Why did Ahmet send three men down to the temple entrance?*

"No more talk, Mr. Froede! Get to the trailer at once." The foreman waved the pistol threateningly.

"Do what he says, Keno," Froede said quickly. "He's gone crazy!" Froede turned and led the way to the trailer-office.

"Inside, quick!" Ahmet commanded as they reached the door.

Froede started up the steps, hesitated, stepped back and waved Keno on before him. Ahmet, startled at first, watched closely as Froede followed Keno up the two steps.

Suddenly Froede kicked back in a circular motion, knocking Ahmet's gun hand to the side. Immediately Froede turned and knocked the tall Egyptian to the ground. The big pistol fell from his hand.

"Quick, Keno!" Froede commanded, "Grab that pistol! We've got to see if the kids are O.K." Drawing his own automatic from his pocket, he began to run toward the tomb entrance.

Just then, two vehicles appeared over the hill from the west. They were moving at high speed, clouds of fine dust rising in the air behind them.

Froede skidded to a stop. He looked for a moment at the cars, weighing the danger of entering the tunnel with strangers approaching behind them. He made his decision at once.

"This way, Keno," he cried. "We can't let them surround us! We must get away if we're to help the kids."

He dashed toward one of the vans with Keno right

behind. The two men jumped in, Froede started the engine, and the van took off. The trailers hid them from the approaching vehicles until they reached a dip in the desert. Here Froede turned behind a small hill of sand, slanted in a southeasterly direction, and poured on speed.

Behind them in the camp, Ahmet lay moaning on the ground, struggling back to consciousness.

Ahmet's three men, meanwhile, had descended the steep steps to the tomb entrance and headed straight for the large stone door. Grabbing its edge, they began to lift it out from the wall.

Deep inside the tomb hallway, David had rejoined his two friends. None of them heard the three men descend the steps.

"What did Uncle Paul want, David?" Penny asked curiously, as the three of them stood in the sphere of light cast by the two lanterns on the floor.

Her face was in shadow. The weird animals on the walls leered down, and again David felt a chill. It felt like a warning and it startled him.

"He wanted to show me a panel," he answered. David didn't break Froede's confidence, but Penny's eyes regarded him solemnly. He realized she wasn't entirely satisfied with his answer.

Mark saved him from further questions. "David, look again at these scenes Keno was translating for us. He's found the treasure chamber!" He spoke in a hushed tone. Sound did funny things in the tomb, and

Mark didn't want to take any chances.

He placed his finger on a series of hieroglyphics. "That's the key!" he whispered. "Keno said these describe the way to the treasure rooms, the pharaoh's tomb and the tomb of his queen, the store rooms—everything!" His eyes gleamed with excitement.

Penny and David looked at him and then at each other. This was the experience of a lifetime!

The massive stone door of the tomb slammed shut with a tremendous explosion, plunging the entrance hall into complete darkness. The sound reverberated down the airtight chamber and rebounded off the far wall.

Mark, Penny, and David whipped around in alarm, shocked by the sudden crash, their ears stunned by the dreadful sound. Looking toward the tomb entrance they saw nothing but blackness.

"Wait here!" David shouted, racing to his pack, which was propped against a wall. He grabbed a flashlight and dashed through the blackness toward the entrance, sprinting after the yellow beam that sliced through the dark void. Several minutes later, David returned. "The door won't budge," he told them.

"What can we do?" Penny asked, forlorn.

"First, we've got to find air," Mark answered, "before we run out."

The darkness closed on them with all the weight of the massive stone building above their heads. The four-thousand-year-old tomb had just become their grave.

CHAPTER 9

THE HIDDEN PASSAGE

"Grab your packs!" David said. "Mark, bring that lantern! I know a way out." He picked up his own pack, whirled, and headed back to the tomb entrance.

"What do you mean?" Mark replied incredulously, lifting his pack and the lamp at his feet. Penny grabbed her pack and camera case and hurried beside him. "How could you know a way?"

"Mr. Froede just showed it to me," David replied over his shoulder. "He said he wanted me to know about it in case something happened to him. Well, it seems that something *has* happened to him—and we'd better get out while we have air to breathe!"

The three of them rushed through the blackness toward the tomb door following the beam of David's powerful light. Their steps echoed against the stone hall as they ran. They came almost to the massive door that closed them in before David veered left, found the open door of the side room, and led them through. Penny followed him, and Mark came last, the lantern in his hand filling the narrow room with light. David rushed to the far wall and set down his pack.

The huge battle scene burst on their sight with awesome effect. "Oh look!" Penny cried out, startled by the vivid warring soldiers, the charging chariots, the dead and dying fighters that were now lit up by the light of the lantern. The desperate warriors seemed alive!

"Quick, Mark! Give me a hand!" David said. His eyes gleamed triumphantly in the lantern light as he knelt before the painting of pharaoh's chariot.

Quickly David found the center of the chariot's wheel and pressed his hand against it. "Push here, Mark!" he commanded. Mark knelt beside him and pushed where David had shown him; he was mystified by David's actions. Penny was too. She leaned over the two boys, staring at the picture of pharaoh's chariot, her lips parted, her heart pounding.

As the boys pushed, a part of the wall slowly swung away from them and into the blackness beyond, swiveling on its hinge. The other end of the stone block began to swing toward them into the room. The block of wall was about four feet high and five feet wide; obviously it was balanced perfectly.

"I'll go first!" David said, picking up his flashlight and crawling into the hole. Inside he flashed the light above him and saw that he could stand, but the tunnel was no more than eight feet high and four feet wide. He stood up and aimed the light straight ahead as he took several steps. The passage ended just a few yards away, but he could see that it turned left. The air was very stale. But it was air!

He walked quickly to the turn. There the passage widened. And it was higher. He turned his beam upward and saw that the ceiling must be fifteen or twenty feet above his head. Shining his light down the passage he couldn't see its end. *How far does it go?* he wondered to himself.

Quickly he rushed back to the opening through which he'd entered, knelt on the cold stone floor, and called to Mark and Penny. "Come on! I've found a passage!"

"Go ahead, Penny," her brother told her. She crawled through the opening, then turned and took the camera case and packs Mark shoved toward her. He handed her the lantern, which illuminated the small passage at once, and crawled in after her.

"These walls are bare!" Penny rose to her feet in wonder at the tunnel they'd found. "I thought the whole inside of this building must be covered with pictures." The space they were in made her think of a long, bare coffin.

"We'd better close this door," David said, "so no one can follow us. Then let's make a mark where we have to push—just in case we have to come back."

He and Mark knelt down and slowly pushed the end of the stone block until it was again flush with the wall. Then David drew his knife and made a series of marks on the soft stone.

Mark had risen and was regarding the narrow tunnel ahead of them with awe. "But where does this lead?" he asked. The lantern flooded the narrow space with light, but the air was stale.

"To the Nile," David replied. "Mr. Froede said this was the passage the ancient Egyptians used to bring things into the tomb when it was built. It leads to long caves that open on the river. Let's go."

"How do we know where we'll come out, David?" Penny asked anxiously, as she followed David to the turn of the passage.

"We don't," David answered. "We'll at least be free though. We can flag a boat and get back to a settlement. Then we can send help for Mr. Froede and the others."

The three of them turned into the larger passage. They walked beside each other in the wider tunnel, Penny between the two boys. Mark's lamp and David's flashlight lit their way.

It was eerie, Penny thought, the three of them walking away from danger, headed they hardly knew where, buried deep undergound, with mummies and priceless ancient treasures probably lying in the rooms they must pass. *Will we be able to get out through the caves at the river?* she wondered. She asked David.

"Mr. Froede thought we could," David replied confidently. "Actually, I think he and Keno know more about this tomb than they told us. I guess they figured we didn't need to know everything."

"The air smells funny!" Mark observed, a little later

"It sure does!" David agreed. "But at least it's air!" He was wondering when this passage would end since Mr. Froede hadn't mentioned the distance to the river. "How far was the river from our camp on the maps?" he asked.

"I don't know," Mark replied.

"I don't either," Penny added.

Suddenly they came to a large battle scene painted in vivid colors on the right-hand wall. "Look at that!" Mark exclaimed in awe, as the huge mural came into range of the lamp he held. Soldiers in marching ranks, chariots with archers, flights of spears and arrows in the air above the warriors, dead and dying men—it was just like the picture in the room through which they'd come.

But David was looking for pharaoh's chariot. When he spotted it, he stopped and pointed it out to Mark and Penny. "Know what's behind that wall?" he asked mysteriously.

"Of course, we don't!" Penny replied. "You're not telling us that *you* do, are you?" She was beginning to feel more relaxed; they all were, in fact.

"Oh, I just have a sense of these things sometimes," he replied with a knowing air. His confidence had shot up at the sight of this painting—just where Mr. Froede had told him it would be!

"O.K., O.K. " Mark broke in, "enough of this. What *is* in there?"

David's face grew serious. "That's the treasure room!"

No one spoke for a moment. Their faces were solemn with the mystery of ancient wonders in the room just beyond the wall as their light shone on the fantastic battle scene before them.

"But we don't go in there unless we have to," David said. "Mr. Froede hoped we could go straight to the river."

"Gosh! I'd love to see what's inside!" Mark said wonderingly.

"So would I," Penny agreed. "Imagine—pharaoh's treasure!"

She looked up at David, her sparkling brown eyes wide with excitement at the prospect of ancient treasures just a few feet away from them! "Think of the necklaces and rings we'd find in there!" For a moment she had forgotten their danger.

"I'd like to see it too!" David replied. "But we'll have plenty of time for that after we get out of here. We'd better hurry."

"But wait!" he said suddenly, turning back to the picture. "We don't know how many other pictures we'll find on these walls! I'll make a mark beside this one, so we can be sure to find it—in case there are others like it. Besides, Mr. Froede said there's another river exit that comes out near the first one."

David took out his knife again, opened the blade, stooped, and made several marks on the floor, just under the picture of pharaoh's chariot. "That should be enough," he said, standing up and replacing his knife.

"Look at it so you can recognize the place if we have to come back."

Mark and Penny looked carefully at his marks. Then the three of them turned and continued down the long passage towards the river. The danger was behind them now—or so they thought!

CHAPTER 10

SEPARATED!

When the trap was sprung, it caught them by complete surprise.

The three of them had been walking down the stone passage, following the light of David's flashlight, wondering among themselves how far they'd have to go to reach the caves.

"At least we can breathe!" Penny observed gratefully. They'd all marvelled at the ancient engineering that had provided for air to move through the tall tunnel from the river. Now they were more confident, but the journey wasn't over and they were still anxious about finding the exit.

"How will we get out when we reach the river?" Mark wondered. "Will there be another picture like the one that let us in here? And what kept robbers from entering the caves and coming through these passages all these years?"

David and Penny couldn't answer these questions. There were too many mysteries to unravel!

Suddenly, the passage turned to the left at a forty-five-degree angle. They followed it, curious, still wondering how far they had to go to get out. And wondering *if* they could get out, once they reached the end.

"Stop!" David said suddenly.

They halted. He shone his light on the floor ahead of them. There, illuminated by the powerful beam, a foot-high stone step stretched across the passage from the walls on each side.

"What's that for?" Mark asked. "If they used this passage to drag heavy coffins and things from the river, why would they want a block like that in the way? It stretches across the whole passage—from one wall to the other!"

"I'm sure they could get over it with ramps," David answered. "And we know they used rollers under heavy things to move them."

"I don't like it," Penny said. "It doesn't seem right." She had a sudden sense of great danger, but she couldn't think of a way to express it.

"It's just a wide stone block like the ones in the wall," Mark replied. He set his lamp down and knelt to study the step. "Wait a minute!" he exclaimed. "It's actually several blocks fit together from wall to wall."

"But why?" David asked. "I mean, what's the purpose of the thing?" His brown eyes were troubled at this strange construction. He looked somberly at Mark for an answer.

"It doesn't matter what its purpose is," Mark replied. "We've got to cross it anyway." He stood up and looked across the raised platform. "It's pretty wide to jump over."

"Well," David said firmly, "if the Egyptians could cross it, we can too. I'll go first." He shouldered his pack.

"No!" Mark said. "My turn—I'll go. You wait here with Penny." He stepped on the foot-high platform and started quickly across.

With a piercing scream of scraping stone, a section of blocks above them hurtled down toward the platform Mark was crossing.

"Watch out!" Penny screamed as the ceiling caved in.

Galvanized by the awful sound and warned by Penny's cry, Mark lunged desperately across. At the same time David grabbed Penny and pulled her back from the ton of falling stone.

The monstrous blocks crashed down on the raised platform just as Mark cleared it on the other side. He raced away from the avalanche of rock that followed. Like a series of exploding shells, they fell to the floor on either side, filling the passage with fine dust.

David pulled Penny farther back, both of them stumbling, choking from the dust, their ears nearly bursting from the crash of stone on stone.

"Mark!" Penny cried, "Mark! Where are you?" Terrified, her eyes filling with tears, she listened for his reply.

"Get back, Penny!" David said, pulling her farther away from the chaos of crashing stone. "It's still falling down!"

"I can't hear him!" she cried. "I can't hear him! Oh, David!" She burst into tears and buried her face in his chest. He put his arms around her, stricken with shock and grief.

But then they heard the faint sound of Mark's voice. "I'm all right, Penny!"

Before either of them could answer, more stones crashed down from the ceiling. But David and Penny couldn't see where they landed. The lamp Mark had set on the floor was buried beneath the fallen rubble. Their only light was the flashlight in David's hand.

David shone the light on the column of collapsed stone and moved the beam upward. The dust was so thick he couldn't see the top of the pile. That, he realized, was why Mark's voice was so faint—the passage was blocked almost to the ceiling. He and Penny could never climb over it!

Then they heard Mark again, fainter now, farther away. "I'm all right. Don't worry. I'll meet you . . . "

Another pile of rock crashed from the high ceiling above, pounding their bruised eardrums, filling the stone passage with thunder and more dust.

"I'm all right . . . , " he said again, his voice so low they could barely hear. Then there was only the sound of loose falling rocks.

Penny sobbed against David's chest as the cloud of fine dust settled around the column of fallen stone. The passage was completely blocked. "Oh, David, I'm so frightened."

"He's safe, Penny," David said. "He got away, but we can't follow him."

Penny nodded her head against his chest. Still she cried as she stood with his arms around her.

"That was a trap!" David said grimly, as he held Penny. "That was a trap set thousands of years ago to catch anyone who came in without knowing. We knew the way—but we didn't know the secret of the trap."

Penny's mind wrestled with the awful implications of David's words. "How many more traps are there before we can get out?" She wiped her tears with her dusty sleeve. She wondered if they would *ever* get out of the tomb. David wondered the same thing.

"I don't know, Penny," he replied miserably.

How many traps remained? There was no way of knowing. His face was deeply clouded with worry at the danger before them. It was up to him to get Penny out alive. Mark was on his own—and so were they.

Suddenly, a deep loneliness fell on him, the loneliness of awful responsibility. How he wished that Mark, with his strength and confidence, were with them now. The darkness engulfed them like a tidal wave. There was only one source of help.

"Penny, let's remember Nehemiah and his friends. They were surrounded by enemies and impossible circumstances. And God delivered them. Let's ask Him to deliver us—and Mark. Nehemiah wasn't alone, and neither are we."

CHAPTER 11

THE CHASE

"They are gaining, Paul," Keno said suddenly. Their van bounced madly across the uneven sand of the desert and slanted toward the high bank of the river to their left. A towering cloud of fine sand thrown up from their wheels followed them.

"I know they are, Keno," Froede replied. "Use the phone and call the base. Tell them what's happened. They've got to get those kids out of the tomb right away!"

Keno searched for the phone under the dashboard. He looked on the floor, then in the glove compartment. "It's gone, Paul," he said, his face stricken. "Ahmet must have taken it."

Froede looked at Keno in disbelief for a moment. His mind raced with the car. They had no way to call for help to rescue the kids. They *had* to escape—but the pursuing vehicle was faster. It was only a matter of time before they were caught!

"How's the gun?" Froede asked.

"I think it's clean," Keno replied. He'd been hastily cleaning the big handgun of the sand that had covered it when Ahmet fell. He'd ripped his handkerchief into small pieces and pulled one of these through the barrel. Then he'd ejected the six big cartridges and wiped them and the chambers into which they fit with great care. Now it was loaded again.

"It's ready, but this is a big gun, Paul," he said wonderingly. "What in the world would Ahmet want with a .357? This weapon would stop a truck!"

Ahmet! Froede's mind wrestled with the truth that his trusted foreman had become their betrayer. "I have no idea!" he replied finally. "But it's obvious he's working for someone else."

Froede and Keno had gained a head start initially by their rapid departure. But the three men who'd closed the tomb door had raced back from the tunnel just as they drove past and must have recognized them.

Indeed the men *had* recognized them! Then they saw Ahmet on the ground and rushed over to help him—just as the two approaching Jeeps roared up to the site and skidded to a stop in a cloud of desert sand.

Hoffmann leaped out while his Jeep was still moving, drew his pistol, and yelled to the three men who now hovered over the crumpled Ahmet. "Who's in that van that just left?"

"Mr. Froede and Keno," one of the men replied.

Hoffmann cursed viciously and turned. Seven other men had stormed out of the Jeeps and rushed to join him. Hoffmann jabbed his finger at their leader, a tall dark-haired giant of a man. "Curt, take your men and bring them back! Alive!"

Curt frowned. "That could be a long chase. And they may be armed. Why don't we just shoot them?"

"You shoot them and I'll shoot *you*!" Hoffmann yelled in violent anger. "Don't argue! We need to know what they've found out about the tomb! And we can't leave dead men and cars with bullet holes all over the desert. The army will be looking for them within two days. That's all the time we have! Get going!"

The big man recoiled before the livid Hoffmann, turned, and ran back with his three men to their vehicle. They jumped in, took off with a roar, and raced after the van.

"Where are the other men in Froede's crew?" Hoffmann said to the men who'd closed the tomb door.

"Two are tied up in that mobile home," one of them pointed. "The rest—the three young people—are shut in the tomb as you ordered."

"Young people?" Hoffmann asked in surprise. "What young people?"

"Two young men and a young woman," the leader answered. "They came with Mr. Froede when he returned. They do the translating for Keno."

Hoffmann's face showed shock at first, then perplexity, as he wrestled with this information. Finally the implications dawned on him, and his tanned face glowed with a vengeful fire. "That's the Daring kids and their friend! The ones who wrecked our plans in Africa. What a coup!" These youngsters had almost ruined his career—and his life! Now he had his revenge! For a moment his hard face was filled with pleasure.

"Get Ahmet up. We have work to do," he commanded.

But they couldn't make Ahmet stand. The writhing man clutched his stomach where Froede had hit him and moaned.

Hoffmann was enraged. "We can't do our work without him!" Furious, he turned around. "Which one of these trailers is the office?"

They pointed and he strode toward it, commanding, "Take Ahmet to his trailer, give him some water, and get him on his feet—before I shoot him!" The three men lifted the moaning Ahmet, carried him to his bunk, and laid him down. His eyes opened, but still he was dazed and couldn't talk.

Hoffmann stormed into the office and read the messages on the fax machine. Digesting them rapidly, he then sat down and typed out a reply to Salin in Cairo, telling of Froede's approaching capture and Ahmet's injury. *We're about to enter the tomb as planned,* he closed before sending the message off.

He paced the narrow room impatiently, waiting for a reply. "What are those fools doing?" he asked himself bitterly. "We've got so little time to pull this thing off!" But the signal arrived a few minutes later, saying his message had been received.

Hoffmann left the office at a fast pace, heading for Ahmet's place. "That Egyptian had better be ready to move!" he said grimly to himself, his mouth a tight slit in his determined tan face. He was in charge of this mission. This time he would not fail!

But across the desert, several miles away now, others were not so confident. Curt, the giant in the pursuing Jeep, urged his driver to greater speed as the four men bounced across the waving sand dunes. Froede and Keno, racing desperately, were still several hundred yards ahead.

"I can't go any faster!" the driver replied, holding grimly to the wheel, never taking his eyes from the dangerously uneven desert before him. "This terrain is terrible! There are rocks and holes everywhere. We'll wreck if I don't see them in time! Besides, we're slowly catching up!"

Curt cursed and eyed the fleeing van ahead. It would be so much easier to fire the automatic rifles and stop the thing in its tracks!

In the van, Froede and Keno contemplated the outcome of this race. "They'll be in shooting range soon," Froede said, glancing at the mirror.

Suddenly the sand dipped. The van left the ground and then bounced hard when it landed. They were rushing down a long incline, parallel to the Nile. Sometimes they could see the wide river between the hills.

"I think the cliffs are steep here," Froede said.

"They are, Paul," Keno replied, as he studied the

river when it showed between the low hills. "I don't see any boats. There's no one we can signal. Even if there were, those men would catch us before a boat could land and pick us up. If it *would* land," he added doubtfully.

Froede made his decision. "We'll have to split, Keno," he said, as he swerved the vehicle away from a jagged pile of rocks. His face showed his concentration on the desert ahead. One more surprise dip or gully and they'd be wrecked! "You'll have to drop me off and keep going."

Keno was shocked! "But you'll be caught! Those men must have rifles, and your pistol would be useless at a distance."

"I was thinking of something else," Froede said. "Quick! Trade guns with me! I'll jump off, then shoot out their engine when they come by. That way, you'll be able to keep going and get help."

Before Keno could object again, he said, "Get out the map. How far is that fishing village? Maybe you can find a radio there."

Keno reached in the glove compartment and retrieved the map. He studied it as the van bounced wildly over the terrain. Finally he found what he was looking for.

"I see it, Paul. I would guess it's seventy kilometers from here. But I can't leave you to be taken by those men." His dark eyes were somber in his long kindly face.

"I won't be taken, Keno," Froede answered firmly.

"I'll hide behind a boulder, shoot out their engine as they come by, then jump down the river bank and run back the way we've come. I'll have a head start on them because they'll follow you until I hit the engine. You'll be long gone, and they'll be too far behind to catch me."

"I don't like it, Paul," the grave Egyptian said. His dark eyes were deeply troubled at the danger this plan held for his friend.

"Neither do I," Froede admitted honestly. "But can you think of another way to get help and save those kids? You must get to that village so you can call our men! And to get you there, I must stop that Jeep!"

Keno couldn't think of a better idea.

Now they were climbing a steeper incline, dust rising far behind them, their pursuers just three hundred yards away. Suddenly they topped the incline and roared through piles of scattered rocks. Hidden momentarily from the Jeep, Froede slowed instantly, weaved around boulders, and then slowed even more.

"Here!" he said quickly, handing over his small automatic. "Give me the revolver!"

The two men traded pistols.

"Take the wheel, Keno! Put you foot on the accelerator as soon as I lift mine. I'll jump out while we're still moving. You take off! God be with you!"

"God be with you, Paul," his friend said, grabbing the wheel and moving closer.

Then Froede leaped out of the moving van, stumbled, almost fell, regained his balance, and raced toward a large clump of rocks near the top of the cliff by the river bank. He crouched down behind them and trained the big pistol on the hill over which the pursuers must come.

Keno moved awkwardly into the driver's seat as the vehicle slowed even more, then poured on the gas. The van leaped ahead just as the Jeep roared over the hill.

Curt spotted the van—much closer that he'd expected. "We've almost got them!" the burly giant exulted. "They've lost ground going up that hill. Hand me the rifle."

"Hoffmann said not to shoot," warned one of the men in back.

"I won't hit them. I'll just scare them into stopping. We've got them now!"

He took the rifle, chambered a bullet, leaned out the window, and took aim.

No one in the Jeep saw Froede as he crouched behind the boulders to their left. He fired the big pistol directly at the radiator of their approaching Jeep.

The racing vehicle plunged by Froede in a cloud of exploding steam. The driver and the rifleman screamed as their vision was blocked by the steam. The Jeep lurched wildly to one side, then to the other, the burned driver fighting to keep it on the road.

As they roared by, Froede turned and shot again. Twice he fired, this time at the spare gasoline tank on the driver's side of the Jeep. The tank burst with the second shot! Fuel sprayed out of the shattered metal container, splashed back along the side of the sputtering Jeep, and reached the exhaust.

Flames flashed from back to front along the whole side of the tortured vehicle. The engine was dead from the heavy pistol slug, but the Jeep was still moving when the men began to bolt from the right-hand doors, leaping to avoid the flames, tumbling into the sand and rocks. The last man jumped from the driverless vehicle just before it smashed into a pile of rocks and exploded. Flames and dark smoke poured into the desert sky, marking the place for miles away.

Froede turned and ran to the edge of the river bank. He began to pick his way down the cliff, amid loose rocks that burned with the heat of the sun. Leaning on the rocks to keep from falling, he scorched his left hand.

His mind was racing. There were three bullets left in his gun. He had no way of knowing how many of the men were still able to chase him, but he couldn't take any chances by waiting to find out! Someone *had* to get away and bring help for those kids who were trapped!

Distracted by these agonizing thoughts, he made a hasty step, his right foot caught in a pile of rock, and pain shot up from his ankle as he fell—and began to slide.

Already a mile away, Keno raced for the fishing village, wondering all the while if he'd find a radio there. If not, where would he go to find one?

His mind flashed back to Mark, Penny, and David. Time was running out in the tomb underground.

CHAPTER 12

WANDERERS UNDER THE SAND

Mark leaped the last three feet to clear the stone step that had triggered the slide from above. The huge block that fell first shattered on the stones below, and one of its pieces struck his shoulder, knocking him to the ground. Falling rocks closed off the light from his lantern behind.

Terrified at the danger, he jumped up and raced away in the nearly total darkness, guiding himself with his hand along the wall. Then he heard Penny's scream. He stopped at once and called back. He'd covered twenty yards or so down the passage, and the stones had ceased falling but the air was thick with dust. "I'm all right, Penny. I'll meet you—"

But his words were drowned by another slide, and he moved quickly on into the utter blackness of the tunnel. Finally he stopped, rummaged in his pack, and retrieved his flashlight. Switching it on, he flashed it back along the passage. Dust hid the column of stone that had fallen when he stepped on the raised stone block on the floor.

I'd better keep going, he thought to himself. *David can lead Penny back to the treasure room, and they can take the other passage. I'll meet them near the river—if Keno read those hieroglyphics right.*

His back hurt behind his left shoulder. Awkwardly he reached his right hand around, felt blood, sighed, and continued down the dark passage. At least he could walk—and run! He'd been scratched before. That wasn't going to stop him.

Mark walked rapidly down the high passageway, wary of another stone block in the path ahead. *Are there any more traps?* he wondered. He flashed the light on the ground and walls ahead as he walked, looking for anything suspicious.

After a while he stopped, reached for his canteen, and took a long drink. *If Mr. Froede had any idea how we'd need this pack!* he thought to himself. He was deeply thankful that Froede had made them take the canteens along every time they went into the tomb just as his father did when they traveled in the bush. "You never know when you might need some of those things," his father had often said. Now Mark knew!

Once again he headed as rapidly as he could down the hall toward the river. He had to get to the exit; he had to meet Penny and David; and they had to get help for Mr. Froede! His mind wrestled with the dangers all of them faced. What was happening to the men who must have been captured above ground? Had Penny been right about Ahmet? Was he the one who'd drawn

Mr. Froede and Keno out of the tomb and ordered the doors to be shut? Wrestling with these chaotic puzzles, Mark moved determinedly through the passage.

Behind him, on the other side of the pile of fallen rock, David had drawn Penny farther away from the collapsed ceiling and the cloud of dust still swirling around it.

"Let's hurry, Penny," he said gently, releasing her from his arms, but taking her hand. "We've got to go back to the treasure room. There's a way to another tunnel on the other side of that room. That's what Mark meant when he said he'd meet us. And don't cry—we know he's safe now."

"I know he is, David, but for an awful moment I thought he wasn't! I couldn't bear it if something happened to him!" Holding tightly to his hand, she walked beside him as they quickly retraced their steps. David flashed his light along the floor and left wall, searching for the battle scene that held the entrance to the treasure room. It seemed to take forever to find it.

"Here we are!" he said triumphantly as they stopped before it. The lurid warfare on the wall now struck them with a more sinister effect. Unlike many of the fallen men pictured on the wall, they'd just escaped death themselves! "Let's open that door."

"David," Penny said suddenly, holding him back, "are we sure there's air in the treasure room?"

David halted. "No, we're not! And if there isn't, we might have trouble crossing the room and trying to open the other side of the wall." He thought about this for a minute, his face puzzled. Then he decided. "We'd better let some air from this passage seep in before we go in ourselves."

He looked at Penny and squeezed her hand. "How many times have you saved us from trouble already!" He tried to show a confident smile, but he couldn't tell its effect because her eyes were deep in shadow.

"I think we've all been helping each other!" she said.

"Well, let's open it and let the air in," he replied. They knelt, found the hub of pharaoh's chariot, and began to push.

Nothing moved!

Startled, but not yet afraid, they pushed harder.

Again the wall didn't budge.

"What's wrong, David?" she asked. They were kneeling close beside each other, the light from the flashlight reflected from the wall. Now he could see the deep alarm in her dark, troubled eyes so close to his own.

"I don't know," he answered. "I guess we have to push harder, that's all. Remember, this wall has been closed four thousand years." Then he had an idea. "Let's try something different!"

He sat on the floor with his feet to the wall. "Sit with your back against mine. Brace your hands and feet on the floor and push your back against me while I push the chariot hub with my feet. That should give me more leverage!"

He put his flashlight on the floor beside him, aimed it toward the wall, and braced his feet against the hub of the chariot. She sat down with her back to his, braced her hands and feet, and pushed as hard as she could against him.

His strength pushed her back! "Try again, Penny!" he said urgently.

The wall didn't move!

They tried again. And again. David moved his heel slightly around the hub, seeking the right place. His hands were braced far behind him on the floor as he leaned for greater pressure against the stone. Again Penny braced herself against his back and strained to support him. Something gave under his feet!

"It moved!" he said exultantly. "Keep pushing!" They pushed again. The stone moved a bit more—then more—then it stuck!

"That's all right!" David said, scrambling to his knees. "Now I can grab the edge and pull." He put both hands around the thin edge that had moved into the passageway and began to pull with all his remaining strength. Slowly a small door in the rock moved. Then it came unstuck with a rush, throwing David back on the floor. At once he got up on his knees. "We did it, Penny! We did it!"

Kneeling in the barely lit passage, noses almost touching, the two grinned at each other, their hearts filled with tremendous joy. The block had swung out—as it was supposed to do! The treasure room was open—for the first time in four thousand years! They had found the entrance that would take them to freedom!

CHAPTER 13

NO WAY OUT

"I'm thirsty!" David said suddenly.

"So am I," Penny answered. "So much has happened—and all so fast! I didn't realize that we'd missed lunch!"

They sat down side by side on the floor beside the open door, backs against the wall, took their canteens out of their packs, and drank gratefully.

"I'm also hungry," David added. "What do we have here?" He rummaged in his pack for the lunch they'd prepared that morning. "It sure looks good," David said before biting into a sandwich.

Penny nodded, her head lowered as she looked over the almonds and dates in her lunch bag.

"Gosh, it feels good to rest for a minute! What a race we've had!" David continued. He thought about Mark for a minute as he ate his sandwich. Then he noticed that Penny was quiet. "Mark has probably reached the end of the passage by now and can take time to eat lunch—like we're doing," he finished lamely. He hoped he hadn't made her worry by mentioning Mark.

"Do you think he'll have any trouble getting out

when he reaches the end of the tunnel?" she asked. That's what they were both worrying about, and that's what neither had wanted to mention.

"Well," David replied confidently, "Mr. Froede showed me the way to open the passageway to the river. He said we could get out that way, so I guess he knew that we could. I think he and Keno knew a lot more than he had time to tell me. He did say that when we go through the treasure room and out that other door, we'll get to the river that way too. I'm sure there's a way out through the caves at the end.

"Also," he added, thinking, "we know about that trap on the floor now, so if we see another one, we'll just jump over it." He finished his sandwich and began on the nuts.

As they sat side by side, eating their lunch, the terrible anxiety of the past hour seemed to seep away. They talked quietly and they both began to relax. An increasing sense of peacefulness came over them.

David decided to save his flashlight batteries. He took one of the light sticks out of his pack, broke it, and set the weird thing down on the floor beside him. It cast a gentle light over everything, illuminating the passage to the left and right.

"What makes those things shine like that?" Penny asked, wondering.

"I don't know," he replied. "They're amazing. This shines for an hour, and it gives a wider beam than a flashlight. It's sort of like a lantern really. We've got a bunch of them in our packs, so we can save our flash-light batteries."

After about ten minutes, David closed his lunch bag and stood. "Let's get going, Penny. We don't want to waste time—or air." He really hated for the peaceful moments to end.

"All right," she replied, closing her pack and getting to her knees. "It's been so nice to have a break." She smiled at him.

They both turned to the wall and prepared to enter the treasure room. David paused. "Penny, this room hasn't been opened for four thousand years. For all that time, no one's seen the things we're about to see!" His face gleamed with excitement. Her eyes shone with the same thought.

The faraway voice from the hall to their right was harsh but clear. "There's a tunnel! This is the way! Now we'll catch those kids!"

David and Penny looked at each other in shock. "They've gotten through the secret door," he whispered. "In there—quick! We've got to douse this light!"

He tossed the light stick into the opening in the wall and shoved her ahead of him. She scrambled through the small opening, he followed, and then they both turned to close the door.

"Let me hide the light first so they can't see it," he said, as he picked up the light stick and stuck it down his shirt. "Now help me close this door."

Together they put their hands on the edge of the door

and pushed. It didn't move.

"It's stuck again," she whispered in anguish. "Oh, David, it's stuck again!"

"Push!" he said. They pushed hard, but it didn't move. They shoved, they pushed, they strained—the stone door didn't budge.

Then they heard other voices from the passageway to their left. More men were crawling through the first door. Soon they would make the turn and come down the passage to the opening—the opening David and Penny could not close!

Far down the passage beyond the column of rock that had poured from the ceiling when he'd sprung the trap, Mark came to a curious formation. He'd been moving rapidly, covering the ground as fast as possible, yet watching carefully for more traps. After a long walk he'd arrived suddenly at a construction against the wall to his right. He saw a narrow series of steps built against the wall, climbing steeply alongside the passage and appearing to level out two-thirds of the way up.

He stopped at once. Was this another trap? He shone his light to the left and right. Nothing else seemed different—just this series of steps built onto the right-hand wall.

I'm not touching those, he said to himself, as he flashed his light into the darkness ahead and proceeded down the hall. But he couldn't help looking up the stairs as he walked by. They led to a narrow ledge, it seemed, and this ledge paralleled the passageway through which he was walking. It was high above the floor, yet seemed to have enough room for someone to walk on it.

That's not for me! Mark said to himself.

But in ten minutes the situation changed dramatically. The passageway came to a dead end! It stopped against a solid wall—a wall that seemed to reach to the ceiling.

How did they get through that? Mark asked himself. Then he remembered—those ancient Egyptians could close up the passageway anywhere they wished, once they'd gotten all the stuff they wanted into the tomb.

But what did Mr. Froede mean by telling David that we could get out this way? Surely there's got to be a way out!

For a long time he stood before the wall that closed the passageway. *There's got to be a way!* he repeated to himself, *or Mr. Froede wouldn't have told David that there was!*

But nothing in the wall ahead, or on the walls to either side, gave any evidence of there being a way out. There was no sign of a door or passage. There was no picture on the wall that might have held a clue. Nothing.

Very reluctantly, he reached a conclusion. *I'll have to go back and go up those steps.* There was clearly no other choice. He turned and walked quickly back the way he had come. When he reached the steps, he looked again at the walls around. But there was no sign of an opening on either side.

Well, here goes. Oh, Lord, please lead me out of here, he prayed.

Then he began to climb the narrow stone steps set out from the right-hand wall. His pack was firmly on his back. His flashlight was in his left hand and with his right he steadied himself as he leaned close to the wall and climbed.

He'd gotten about two-thirds of the way up the wall, when the steps levelled out and a narrow ledge ran along the side of the wall. He paused and took stock of the situation. He had no choice but to go on. Carefully, leaning against the wall to avoid falling, he moved along the narrow way, gingerly placing one foot ahead of the other.

The walk on this knife-like path seemed to last forever—in fact, it took fifteen minutes to reach the end. The end was a wide opening, not easily visible from the ground below. This opening ran the width of the passageway, and was no more than four feet high. Mark stopped before it. He'd been feeling a breath of air for several minutes; now he knew where it came from!

I've reached the entrance! he said exultantly to himself. *Mr. Froede was right! I've made it! Oh, thank you, Lord!*

Gratefully he took off his pack and shoved it into the opening ahead. Light was coming from the wide slash in the wall—light, he figured, from the sun outside! But the light from ahead threw into shadow the surface of the stones just in front of him, and he couldn't see any details.

Mark pulled his body carefully onto the stone shelf and thrust his flashlight directly before him. He was elated! In just a few minutes, he'd be at the river—and outside!

Shocked from sleep by the sudden intrusion, the startled cobra struck!

CHAPTER 14

THE NOOSE TIGHTENS

Paul Froede slid finally to the bottom of the cliff in a cloud of loose rock and red dust. His body was bruised all over and his clothes torn by the sharp rocks; he bled from a dozen cuts. Pain shot from his ankle.

For a few moments Froede lay on his back in the rock and settling dust, still gripping the pistol, collecting his strength. Then, with great difficulty, he rolled over and struggled to his knees.

He thought he'd seen a boat as he'd whirled round and round on his slide down the cliff. Looking intently at the river, he found the craft he sought. A large white speedboat cruised leisurely along the Nile, close to the bank on which Froede had come to rest.

Wiping the blood from his face with his torn sleeve, the bruised and battered man got painfully to his feet and waved at the boat.

The two men in the pleasure craft had stared, fascinated, as he fell and were looking at him now. They waved back—but the boat did not turn.

Keeping his gun low in one hand, Froede beckoned

them towards him with the other.

They waved again and then looked straight ahead as they continued on their course up the Nile, moving to his right. The sleek white boat with blue trim and a smart flag at the bow would soon be out of sight!

Froede brought up the heavy pistol, rested his right hand in his left, aimed, and fired. The heavy slug threw up water just in front of the boat, in clear sight of the two men.

Instantly the man at the wheel turned the boat to the left, swerved out into the Nile, and increased speed!

Outraged, Froede took careful aim and fired directly to the left and front of their course. The slug kicked up another great spout of water and skipped out into the river, making splash after splash until it finally sank. He fired again, but this time he aimed deliberately for the rising bow of the speeding craft. The heavy bullet tore through the woven plastic and sent splinters flying into the air!

The men got the message! Spinning the boat back to the right and heading toward Froede, the man who was steering reduced speed. His companion threw his hands in the air and waved frantically to Froede to stop shooting.

Froede stopped. He had to—his gun was empty! But the men on the boat didn't know that. So he aimed at them with grim determination as they brought the boat to shore just below a ledge of rocks. Then he dropped the barrel slightly—he didn't want them to see that the chambers were empty—and limped painfully across the rock ledge to the water.

The steersman held the bow of the boat while Froede lowered himself to the deck with difficulty. Pointing the gun downward, almost negligently, he moved slowly across the bow to the glass windshield, eased carefully around this, and climbed painfully into the enclosed space. Waving the pistol, he motioned the men away from him.

His body was covered with dust and blood and his clothes torn, but his blue eyes blazed with implacable determination. All in all, he presented a terrifying figure to the yachtsmen and they quailed in fear before him. The man behind the wheel was tall and overweight; his companion was stocky, powerfully built, and wore a white cap. Under more pleasant circumstances, they were probably very nice guys, Froede thought to himself. These were not pleasant circumstances.

"Do you speak English?" he asked, his big pistol aimed leisurely at their feet.

"Non, monsieur. Nous parlons francais," the man behind the wheel replied.

"Très bien," Froede answered in flawless French. "Vite! Vite! Head to the middle of the river! Then go north!" He waved the pistol, careful to keep the barrel low so they couldn't see it was empty.

"Oui, monsieur," the man answered anxiously, backing the boat, turning it again into the river, and shoving the throttle forward.

The powerful craft leaped ahead so suddenly that Froede almost fell overboard! Grabbing the gunwale he steadied himself, then sank down in a canvas chair near the stern. The two men huddled close together by the instrument panel, clearly anxious to please.

The boat's speed increased as it raced away from the high cliff. *A rifleman could pick us to pieces,* Froede thought. He still didn't know if anyone had escaped from the burning Jeep, and he couldn't take a chance of remaining in rifle range of any who might have survived.

In a few minutes he waved the gun and ordered the driver to change course to the north. Then he fumbled for his wallet with his left hand, set this in his lap while he held the gun in his right, and proceeded to extract two cards.

"Do you have a radio?" he asked the stocky man.

"Oui," the man replied, pointing to the instrument attached to the panel near the wheel.

"Call the Cairo police and ask for the officer on this card," he said, holding out both cards. "Read my name from this other one, and tell him I need help at once!"

Puzzled at the turn of events, the man approached gingerly. *This gunman wants me to call the police!* he thought. He glanced fearfully at the big pistol, took the two cards, and returned to the radio.

To Froede, it seemed to take forever to send the message. The white waves curled back from the bow on either side of the boat, the shore moved past, an empty flat barge pulled by a tug passed to their right. Froede was struck by the appearance of the barge with the tall bridgeworks.

Finally, the radio crackled an answer. The man spoke for a minute and then said, "He wants to talk to you."

Froede struggled to his feet, held the rail in his left hand as he moved forward, then leaned against the boat's side, and took the radio phone. The stocky man stepped carefully away.

"Froede here," he said. He listened for a moment, and then his worried dusty face broke into a smile. "Am I glad to hear your voice, Colonel!"

Very briefly he told of the assault, the trapping of the youngsters, and his flight over the desert with Keno. "You'll find the wrecked Jeep by looking for the smoke," he said grimly. "But you've got to get my team together and rescue those kids."

After a few more words, he handed the radio phone to the man who'd made the connection for him. Carefully avoiding the gun, the man took the phone, listened to the colonel, agreed excitedly, and hung up. He smiled at Froede.

Froede tossed the pistol into the nearest canvas chair and held out his hand to shake that of his former prisoner. "Do you have anything I can drink?" he asked as he sank back into the deck chair.

"Oui! Oui! Mais certainement!" the man replied eagerly, glad to know that he and his friend were not prisoners of a gangster. He went below and returned with a cold bottle which he handed the exhausted American.

Froede grinned his thanks and drank deeply. He gave the man his business card. "Call me next week. I'll pay for the hole in your boat. And I apologize. But how else could I have stopped you?" he asked, shrugging like a native Frenchman.

The men were all smiles. *How else indeed?*

Then Froede changed his plan. "Can you take me back past the place where you found me?"

"But of course!" the tall man replied, spinning the wheel.

At once the boat changed course, swerved gracefully around, and headed south, back toward the shore near the buried tomb. The craft increased speed. High curving waves of white water rose from each side, the tops blown gently toward the west by the strong breeze that swept across the river.

They passed that strange barge again. Froede wondered why it was moving so slowly. Then he saw to their left a thick cloud of dark smoke from burning fuel rising high into the air, also blown westward by the wind from the Nile.

CHAPTER 15

DECISIONS AND DILEMMAS

Hoffmann strode vigorously toward the mobile home where Ahmet had been taken. *He'd better be ready to help!* he said grimly to himself. Bursting into the Egyptian's quarters, he found Ahmet sitting on his bunk, holding his head in his hands. The two men beside him snapped to their feet when Hoffmann came into the room.

"How is he?" Hoffmann demanded.

"He's better," one of the men replied. "He can talk."

"Then talk and talk fast!" the angry German answered. "We're two days late—thanks to those bunglers in Paris! And time's running out. Tell me what you've done!" He stood threateningly before the recovering man.

Slowly Ahmet sat straighter and began to outline the situation. He described how they'd tied up two of Froede's men, sealed the three youngsters in the tomb, and captured Froede and Keno. "But they surprised us," he said fearfully. "They knocked me down and got

100

away in the van."

"I know they got away, you fool!" Hoffmann answered. "But we'll get them. My men are chasing them now. They'll bring them back and we'll get the information we need."

"We don't need them anymore," Ahmet said quickly, glad he could contribute something to placate the angry European. "The men in Paris faxed me the data we wanted. They finally read the hieroglyphic stone in the Louvre and learned all we need to know."

He stood up slowly, testing his strength, eager to please the volatile Hoffmann. His face broke into an ingratiating smile. "I know the signs that show the secret passageways to the treasure room! Inside that, we'll find the larger doors that open to the tunnels to the river. The boat can come in at dark tonight, and we'll have the tunnel exit open for them."

Hoffmann's icy stare showed no signs of thawing. But Ahmet knew the German had to be pleased.

"We've done it!" the Egyptian concluded triumphantly.

"Not yet we haven't!" Hoffmann objected, whirling and striding toward the door. "Not until we get into that treasure room and then open the tunnel exit for the men in the boat. Not until they take out all the treasure they can carry, and not until we get away to the landing down the Nile, and unload the treasure in the trucks that wait for us. *Then*—and not until then—will we have finished the job!"

He jumped down the trailer step to the sand, and the

others followed him. His three men were waiting by the Jeep. Hoffmann turned back to the tall Egyptian behind him.

"Ahmet, we'll have to open the tomb now. We can't wait for those kids to suffocate. One of my men will guard them with a gun while we find the treasure room. I want that treasure and I'll not leave without it. When we've gone out to the river, we can shut them in—with Froede and Keno and their workers—and let them all die!"

"You!" he pointed to one of Ahmet's men. "Stand guard in the office. If the phone rings or a fax message comes, don't answer—come tell me at once. Do you understand?"

The man cowered before Hoffmann's blazing eyes. "Yes, sir!" He turned and ran towards the office.

"Let's go," Hoffmann said, striding rapidly toward the steep steps that led to the tomb entrance below. "After we open the tomb, you," he nodded to the man beside him, "will guard those kids. The rest of us will go through the passage to the treasure room. We've got to open the larger doors and then make sure the entrance at the river is passable for the men on the barge."

They raced down the steps, four of them pulled open the heavy door, and all moved in carefully, their guns ready, looking for Mark, Penny, and David.

"You two go in that room there!" Hoffmann ordered. "The rest fan out and cover this hall."

All the men had flashlights. They moved down the hall in a line abreast. At the end they found the fantastic mural on the wall. But there was no sign of the youngsters!

"Are they in that room?" Hoffmann yelled, running back to the entrance to the small room beside the hall.

"No one's there," his men replied. "The place is empty."

Hoffmann raged. "But where could they go?" he demanded.

"Froede must have told them of the secret passage," Ahmet replied, quivering with fear. "There's no other way they could have left because we shut these rooms when we captured Froede and Keno." His long face showed his worry. *Could those kids find their way out of the tunnel to the river?* But he was afraid even to mention this possibility to the angry German.

He didn't have to. "Quick, then!" Hoffmann yelled. "They've got a start on us! They might escape before we can catch them. They could ruin everything—again!" he raged.

Turning to the trembling Ahmet he demanded, "Lead us to that secret passage. We must catch them!"

Ahmet ran into the small room, turned his flashlight on the mural of the great battle scene, and searched for the key he'd been told about in the fax message. The irate Hoffmann standing beside him rattled him badly and made concentration difficult. Finally he found the chariot of the pharaoh and the hub of its wheel.

"This is it! Help me push!" he exclaimed.

One of Hoffmann's men knelt beside him, the two together pushed against the stone, and the block swung open! The dark void opened to their view.

"Get in there!" Hoffmann ordered.

The man beside Ahmet retrieved his light, pulled a pistol from his belt, crawled quickly in, and disappeared from sight. They heard him rise and take several steps. Then he called triumphantly. "There's a tunnel! This is the way!"

Far down the passage, on the other side of the fallen pile of rock, at the very end of the tall tunnel in fact, Mark faced mortal peril.

The light was smashed from his hand. All Mark did see was the blur of the deadly snake as it flashed by, its teeth snagged by the thin metal rim of the flashlight. Before he could realize the full terror of what had grazed him, he heard the heavy flashlight strike the stone floor below, followed by the thud of the reptile's body he'd barely seen.

Now his heart pounded with the flood of adrenalin that poured into his blood! He lay on the narrow edge, unable to see any details on the stone's surface ahead of him. The diffuse light from the wide opening before him—the light that had just a moment before given him such hope—now threatened death. How many more snakes were ahead of him on this ledge? His body was suddenly drenched with sweat. For a moment he couldn't move.

Finally he gathered himself and rose slowly and carefully to his knees. *I've got my pack as a shield,* he thought. Also, he remembered that he had light sticks. Reaching into the pack with his hand, he fumbled until he found one of them and slowly brought it out.

What will I see when I break this thing? he wondered fearfully. But he had no choice. He *had* to see what was ahead of him on the ledge if he were to get out of this underground complex.

He broke the light stick and held it away from his body. The light began to glow; then it shone around him and onto the ledge ahead. There were no other snakes in sight! He began to crawl toward the opening.

He saw that the ledge was even wider than it first appeared. Looking to his right, he thought, *That's where Penny and David might come out!* He stopped. *Maybe I should go look for their tunnel.*

Kneeling in the low constricted stone chamber, he wrestled with his choices. The dim light ahead must be coming from the entrance to the caves so he'd almost reached the outside. Yet what could he do by himself if he got out? Attack the camp alone? Not much likelihood of success there!

But if he found David and Penny, together they might be able to get back to Mr. Froede and Keno. Also, David and Penny might not know what to do if their tunnel had steps along the wall like the ones he'd taken. They might think it was another trap—as he had at first. And if they finally decided to climb the stairs, they wouldn't be expecting snakes when they came to the ledge. They had to be warned.

He began to crawl to his right in the narrow space, searching for an opening like the one from which he'd come. The low ceiling of the ledge made him feel trapped. *Gosh, how I hate being cooped up!* he said to himself. Crawling slowly along the wide stone ledge— light stick in his left hand, pack on his back, and looking for snakes—he prayed silently, *Lord, keep me calm!*

Finally he saw it! He moved carefully to the hole in the stone. Looking down, the glow from his light stick showed him stairs along the wall to his left, just like the ones he'd climbed. This was the tunnel Penny and David would come through when they got out of the treasure room! *If* they got out.

CHAPTER 16

THE TREASURE OF PHARAOH!

Far back down the tunnel Mark had just left, the voice of the men emerging from the secret passage struck terror into the hearts of David and Penny. Nothing they had tried to do had moved the stone door an inch. But if they didn't close it at once, they'd be captured and probably killed!

David's heart was broken as he confessed defeat. "I can't move it, Penny!" David said despairingly, as they both shoved with all their strength against the low block. "I can't move it!"

They were on their knees, side by side, straining desperately against the edge of the stone door. Penny's heart was racing with fear, but she turned her head and looked into David's anguished eyes just inches from her own.

"Yes, you can, David," she told him with all the confidence she could muster. "And you will—I know you will." *Oh God, help David move the door,* Penny prayed to herself.

He looked at the brave girl for a moment as the voices from the hall became louder. He remembered the trust she'd placed in him and Mark when Hoffmann's men forced them into the path of the crocodiles. He seemed to gather resolve.

He stood up. "I'll try something else." Turning his back to the stone block, he gripped it with both hands. He leaned backward over it and, bracing his feet against the floor, strained with all his strength against the edge of the stone door that protruded into the room. His muscles bulged beneath his shirt.

Slowly the block began to swing toward the wall! He shoved again. Penny crawled beside him and pushed as hard as she could. Adrenaline pumped in their veins as the race against capture and death moved with infinite slowness. But the block continued to move until finally the opening was completely closed!

Utterly exhausted, the two sat on the floor, their backs against the door they'd just shut. Penny reached for David's hand and squeezed. He squeezed back, too exhausted for a moment to speak. He took the light stick out of his shirt and placed it on the stone floor.

"Thank God!" he said finally. "Thank God for His mercy! I couldn't have closed that, Penny—not even with your help." He looked at her in the dim glow and saw relief on her lovely face. She rested her head against his shoulder.

As his strength began to return, he realized they were not yet safe. "We've got to get something in front of that door so they can't shove it open!"

He released her hand, rose to his feet, and searched frantically for something to roll against the stone door through which they'd just come. David's eyes fell at once on a row of jars beside the wall. More than four feet high, they must have held supplies for the pharaoh and his family on their supposed journey into the next world.

"Hold the light, Penny. I'll try to move these jars against the door!"

She took the stick from his hand. He grabbed the top of the nearest jar—filled with he knew not what—tipped it toward his body and struggled to roll it along its bottom rim to the secret door. Slowly the heavy thing moved. Finally he had it against the wall and set it down. It slammed tight against the door.

David dashed back for another of the jars and rolled it carefully to join the first. The things were almost too heavy for him to handle! Somehow he managed to get four jars lined up against each other and jammed against the side of the door that opened into the room.

"I don't think they'll open that now," he said, gasping for breath, his chest heaving from the exertion. "There's too much weight against the door's edge. They won't have any leverage on the other side to move it against all that weight."

Penny had been holding the light stick while he'd moved the jars. Now she handed the light to him as he turned from the door. Taking the light in his right hand, he turned to face the vast stone room and took her hand in his. She moved closer to him and together they gazed for the first time on the treasure of the pharaoh.

The splendor took their breath away! Before them was a ship, intricate in design, marvelous in workmanship, its mast stepped and sails furled. To the left and right of the ship were tall figures made of stone—or maybe wood. Surrounding them on every side, as far as they could see in the dim glow of the light stick and over their heads on the ceiling, were paintings of marvelous and sinister design!

The zodiac paced in stately fashion over their heads with its various constellations as they'd been seen by mankind for thousands of years. David handed Penny the light stick, slipped off his pack, and took out his flashlight. Turning it on the ceiling, he gasped at the colorful detail. The sun god in his chariot marched across the heavens on his eternal rounds.

"David, look!" Penny said, holding his hand tightly and pointing to her left. There two massive figures towered against the shadowed wall beyond, their solid manly torsos crowned with the heads of giant crocodiles. Their sinister gaze was directed at a spot behind the boat.

"Let's see what's on the other side," he said, leading her by the hand around the ship.

Suddenly they were overwhelmed by a sense of ancient evil. They both felt it—ancient evil and present menace! Those gods were somehow *real*—not sovereign they knew—but *real* nevertheless. They were as real as the demons Jesus had cast out of troubled Galileans, real as the evil that caused the murders and horrors and wars of today.

Fearfully David and Penny walked around the ship. Their lights displayed a huge sarcophagus standing in the middle of the room. Statues of gods and men and animals were faced toward it. A massive gold-crowned head rose from one end of the long coffin. The pharaoh! The outline of his gold-encased body rose dramatically above the surface on which it lay. His hands were crossed, the rods of his authority held firmly in his grip.

They couldn't move. The slightest motion of their bodies and the lights they held made the shadows of the statues of men and gods and animals move across the walls beyond. The motion of these shadows brought upon them an unearthly dread, a vague but powerful fear, a mix of wonder and malice, of beauty and demonic threat. Their awe at the spectacular beauty had changed. There was spiritual menace in these ancient gods.

"Let's go, Penny!" David said suddenly. "This is no place for us!" Holding her hand he led her toward the other side of the room. "Let's find that mural and get out."

They passed casks and statues of soldiers and servants until they came to the far wall. There before them was the familiar scene: the pharaoh's chariot crushing the soldiers of the enemy legions beneath its wheels. Kneeling quickly before it, they pressed the hub of the chariot's wheel. Would this door stick as the other had?

It opened at the first touch as if it moved on newly oiled hinges! They looked at each other in deep relief.

"Wait here, Penny," David said. "I'll go in first."

He crawled through the opening and stood up. Flashing his light on the walls and ceiling, he saw that these too were bare. Satisfied, he turned back to the small door.

As soon as David disappeared into the opening to the tunnel, Penny felt again the menace of the evil gods whose images filled the treasure chamber. Fearfully she glanced back at the looming statues. Her eyes fell on the crocodile-headed beast that leered directly at her; she shuddered.

"Come on, Penny!" David's voice reached her through the opened port. "It's just like the tunnel on the other side of the treasure room."

Quickly she crawled through and stood beside him.

"Let's close this—just to keep things neat," he said. They pushed the stone until it was flat against the wall. On this side also there was the familiar painting with the battle scene and chariot of pharaoh. He took her hand in his, and they started rapidly down the long tunnel toward the river.

"I'll be so glad to get out of here, David," Penny

said as they moved through the dark passage, guided by the light stick in her hand and the flashlight in his.

"So will I," he agreed solemnly. "These idols scare me. They're so threatening. I can't explain it. They're evil, that's all!"

He wondered why he felt such danger from the statues. "It's one thing to look at idols in the museum, but it's different being locked up with them, surrounded by them!"

The journey seemed long and their feet heavy as they walked through the dark hall. They were completely surprised when suddenly they came to narrow steps that rose along the right-hand wall to what appeared to be a ledge above.

"Is that another trap?" Penny asked, shuddering.

"I don't know," he replied. "Let's check the walls and floor and see if anything else looks suspicious." He flashed the beam carefully along both walls and all over the floor ahead. Nothing looked different from the path they'd already trod.

"I wonder if we're supposed to go up those steps, David?" she asked finally.

"I'd hate to take a chance, Penny—not unless we have to. Let's keep going."

Puzzled and aware that danger could strike them any minute, they walked on through the tunnel. When they finally reached the end they found—as Mark had—nothing but a blank wall!

"What in the world!" David exclaimed, looking at

the wall of stone blocks that rose from floor to ceiling, completely sealing the tunnel. "How are we to get through *that*?"

"The Egyptians must have," she replied, "or they couldn't have brought all those things into the tomb."

"But then they sealed it up—at least it looks like they did." He moved closer. "Maybe we're supposed to press one of these stones to open a door or something."

"Be careful, David," Penny said anxiously, pulling him back. "We don't want to take a chance. Remember the stones that fell on Mark!"

"Well, there's nothing here anyway," he said, "no picture, no design. It's all flat blocks fitted together." He was completely mystified.

"I guess we'll have to go back to those steps," he said reluctantly. "I don't see any other choice. Do you?" He looked at her, his eyes showing profound disquiet at the prospect.

"No," she replied in a low voice. "There's no other choice. Oh, David!" She leaned her head against him. He put his arms around her, and they stood silently for a moment in the dark of the ancient passage, over-whelmed by the uncertainties ahead.

After a minute he spoke. "Penny, the Lord's protected us so far. We'll have to trust Him now." He managed a smile as he stepped back and she managed one in return. They turned and walked back toward the steps.

When they reached the steps David again inspected them closely with his light. "These sure are narrow—

but they seem sturdy enough."

"I hate heights, David," she admitted.

"And I hate being cooped up!" he said. "We'll just have to be careful."

He thought about it for a moment as he studied them. "You go first; that way, I can grab you if you feel unsteady. Put the light stick in your belt, face the wall if you like, use both hands for balance, and ease up a step at a time. Stand straight and lean against the wall. I'll be right behind you. Just look at the wall—not at the floor of the tunnel. O.K.?"

"All right," she replied bravely. She put the stick partway in her belt so the top half threw light ahead of her, and slowly began to climb the steep ascent.

Putting his flashlight in his pocket, David moved right behind her, his left hand on her back as he followed her up the steps. His hand was steady as they moved.

"How're we doing?" he asked when they'd gone a dozen steps.

"Fine, I think," she replied, more confident now. "We're almost halfway up." She looked upward to the ceiling that was now not so far away.

"We're getting there," he agreed. And soon they had. "Now just step up on the ledge. I'll follow, and we'll be out of here!"

"David, look at that light ahead!" she exclaimed. "I think we're almost there!"

They moved along the narrow ledge, his hand still on her back, giving her confidence.

"I thought you'd never get here!" her brother's voice boomed from the vaguely lighted area ahead.

"Oh! Mark!" she cried.

"Careful!" David warned. "Don't lose your concentration!"

They inched forward until they came to the opening. Mark reached for Penny with his strong arms, lifted her up, and pulled her into his bear hug. David climbed up and joined them. Penny was crying with joy and relief.

CHAPTER 17

ON THE NILE

On the speeding white boat, Froede looked back at the long barge that moved down the Nile, close to the western bank. *What is that thing doing here?* he wondered. *Why is it going so slowly?* He asked his new friend to steer their boat gradually toward the western shore of the river. "Keep it slow so they won't notice us from that barge," he said, gesturing behind him.

In a few minutes the black smoke from the still burning Jeep came into sight above the cliffs to their left. Froede wondered how many of the men it had held were still able to give trouble?

"I think that fire is about nine miles from here," he told the two Frenchmen. "That's where you can let me off."

"But what will you do on foot?" they asked. They had no idea what was going on, but they knew this bloodied man was on the side of the police.

"I'll think of something," he replied with his usual grin. "And it had better be good!" he said quietly to himself. His only weapon was the empty pistol tucked into his belt.

They passed out of sight of the barge as the river

bent slightly. After a short while the stocky man turned to Froede. "We are as near that smoke as we can get, but the river bank is steep. Are you sure you want to get off by those cliffs?"

Froede had been looking at the cliffs for some time. What a perfect place for the tunnels to the tomb to end—or begin! The entrances had to be above the water level of the river in case of flooding. Yet they had to be accessible as well. This was as good a place as any, and it seemed to be directly opposite where the tomb should be. He could make a quick search for Mark, Penny, and David. If he didn't find them, he'd head for the camp and see what damage he could do to the barbarians who'd overrun it!

"That's the spot," he replied.

Finally out of sight of the barge, the speedboat slanted directly toward the shore, moving under the curiously formed cliffs. Froede could see openings vanish into darkness under the cliff's overhanging ledge. Somewhere in those openings must be the entrances to the tunnels!

"My friends, you've been wonderful! I need two final favors. Continue steering this same way so the men on that barge don't get suspicious at your change of course. And call the colonel again. Tell him I'm worried about that barge."

"Certainly," they agreed.

The boat touched shore under the cliffs. Froede limped out on the deck and jumped the short distance to the soft sand. Then he turned and waved as the craft pulled away and continued down the Nile. Already one of the men was on the radio phone to Cairo.

Froede didn't have much time before the barge would come into sight. He limped along the shore, looking up into the openings, wondering which led to caves and which were merely gaping holes in the rock's face. In some places he could climb up to check; others were too steep, or the red rocks too loose for footing. His swollen ankle throbbed but he struggled on.

Finally, he gave up. *I'll never be able to find it from this end,* he realized. The ancient builders would have made it as difficult as they possibly could to keep out invaders. Or, coming from the inside, the kids might have gotten out already. In that case, what would they have done?

He wrestled with his choices and regretted that he hadn't asked the colonel when the police would reach the camp. If the kids got back there before the police, they could get hurt.

I'll head to the camp, he decided. *If I can just get in our quarters, I'll have another gun—one with bullets!* He searched the cliff's face, found a place that looked possible to climb, and began the steep and difficult ascent. His ankle felt awful, but he had to keep going.

A hundred yards to the left of him, but still underground, Mark, Penny, and David were about to exit the tunnel. The passageway had narrowed or the walls had collapsed in years long past. They crawled now, the packs on their backs scraping the low ceiling, Mark pushing his ahead in case more snakes should be waiting.

Finally they came to a hole in the stone surface. The three gathered around the opening and stared down. They saw water below!

"That's the river!" David said, "At last!"

"But how will we get down?" Penny asked.

"We could drop," Mark suggested. "But we don't know how deep it is. How far down would you say it is?"

"About thirty feet," David replied.

To their left and right they found a series of openings in the stone surface. Some of these were blocked up; several were open; some looked down on water. All were very narrow. Mark would have a tight squeeze going through any of them.

As they peered through another and began to wonder how they'd get out, Penny suddenly exclaimed. "Look! A rail!" She pointed.

There was a rail! Imbedded in rock, angling downward from the opening through which they were looking, a round iron rail led out of sight to the water below.

The two boys looked at each other. "Let me try it, Mark," David volunteered. "You're so fat and heavy you might pull the whole thing down!" He tried to grin.

Mark objected, but David insisted. "It's our best bet. One of us has got to try it. I'm lighter than you are."

Mark had to agree finally.

David took off his pack and then his shoes. He lowered his head and arms into the hole and gripped the rail while Mark held his legs. "O.K.," he said, "I've got it. Let go."

Penny held her hands to her cheeks as she watched him crawl headfirst through the hole. Fervently she prayed. Mark let go of David's legs, and he began to crawl downward. Quickly David caught his feet around the rail; hanging upside down, he moved out of their sight.

They heard his body scrape slowly along, hands and feet wrapped around the rail, on a slanting path downward. Then he stopped moving.

"I'm at the end," he said. "I'll drop from here."

"Be careful, David!" Penny cried out.

"Don't worry," he called. Letting his feet down, he hung from the rail by his hands, slowly extended his arms—and dropped! They heard him splash in the water below.

The long moment was agonizing—actually it was a few seconds—before his head popped to the surface a few yards out. "It's O.K.," he called triumphantly. "This pool's deep! And I can see the river! We've made it!"

He swam back until he was almost directly under them. "Toss me the packs, one at a time, and I'll put them on a ledge here."

Mark lowered the packs, including Penny's camera case, one at a time and dropped them to David in the water below. He caught each one before it hit the water, swam with it to shore, and swam back for the next.

"Penny," he called up, "crawl out on the rail as far as you can, then hang down, and drop. I'll be right here to pull you up out of the water!"

"I can't crawl upside down for long, David," she said.

"You won't have to! I'll be right beside you when you land. Come on in; the water's fine," he tried to joke.

She hugged her brother for courage and then stuck her face and arms down through the hole. He held her legs as she crawled downward, gripping the rail with her arms. Slowly she moved down the rail. "Let go of my right leg, Mark," she said. He did so, and she hooked her ankle around the rail.

"Let go, Mark!" Quickly she brought her left ankle around the rail also and began to crawl down for a few feet. "I can't hold on any longer, David!" Her voice was tense.

"Let your feet down—one at a time so you don't pull yourself off the rail—and hang down. Then take a deep breath, hold it, and drop," he called reassuringly.

She lowered her feet, hung for a moment, and took a deep breath. Then she released her grip and plunged with a splash into the water below!

David went under when she hit, grabbed her out-stretched arm, and pulled her quickly to the surface. She came up spluttering. Holding her waist with one arm, he treaded water while she got her breath. Then she smiled a huge smile of relief. "I can swim now!"

she said. He let her go, and they swam a few yards to the ledge where he'd stashed their packs.

Mark followed with a huge splash; then he swam over to join Penny and David. The three of them held to the projecting ledge and looked at the hole from which they'd come. It was difficult to spot without any heads peering down!

"No wonder no one's found this place!" Mark exclaimed. "There's no floor here to stand on and climb from, and you can't even see there's an opening above to explore! I wonder where the main tunnel opens on the river. There has to be a bigger entrance if they took in all those things from boats."

"I don't know," David replied, "but I think we'd better get going." They retrieved their packs; then, holding on to the rough rocks projecting from the wall, they worked their way along the rocky ledge, holding their packs and Penny's camera case above water to keep them from getting any wetter than they already were. One by one they came out the opening into the brilliant sunlight. There, before them was the Nile!

"Look! There's a boat!" Penny exclaimed, pointing to her left.

The boys looked where she pointed and saw a craft speeding down the Nile. "It's too far for us to signal," Mark said, discouraged. "But where there's one, there'll be more!"

"We can climb out here," David said, pointing to a series of rocks that could serve as steps. He led the way, Penny followed, and Mark came last. Slowly they crawled up the slanting rock surface, gradually coming to the top of the cliff that overhung the river. At the top, they rested and looked at the water below. They'd made it this far!

CHAPTER 18

ACROSS THE DESERT

Keno drove skillfully, speeding where he could, slowing down when the ground ahead became too rough or uncertain. The last thing he wished to do was break an axle! If he did that who knows how long he'd be stranded? How then could he bring help to the youngsters in the tomb? He had to be careful.

But he had to be fast! He drove with total concentration, weaving around piles of rock, sticking to the harder patches of sand, avoiding the deep dunes where he might get stuck. He drove for what seemed like an eternity before he encountered the narrow hardened road that led from the southwest to the village.

Relieved at the sight of the roadway, he swerved onto it and increased speed. He wondered as he drove what had become of Paul Froede; he'd seen the smoke from the burning Jeep climbing in the sky behind him and knew that Paul had succeeded in stopping their pursuers. But had he gotten safely away himself? How many men survived that burning Jeep? Would they find Froede with their long-range rifles before he could get away?

Keno's mind was filled with these and other dark thoughts as he raced across the desert. Above all, he wondered if anyone in the village ahead had a radio. Everything depended on that; he *had* to find a radio and call Cairo to send rescue teams for the kids underground, for Froede, and for the other loyal workers whom he hadn't seen since Ahmet had first pulled a gun.

Before he realized it, the village grew in the distance, its image waving curiously in the rising heat from the desert. As he neared the houses, he saw a building with a radio tower! His long face broke into a great smile of joy.

Far behind him, Paul Froede had succeeded in reaching the top of the cliff above the Nile. His ankle was killing him. The soreness of his bruises was worse. But his sharp mind was on the task ahead. How could he reach the camp without being seen? How could he radio for help without getting caught? Above all, how could he rescue the kids buried in the tomb?

He rested for a few minutes, favoring his swollen ankle, catching his breath, gathering his thoughts. The resolve in his bright blue eyes never wavered, however, and soon he was moving carefully across the desert, limping and weaving on a course that kept him off the skyline and between the dunes. He knew where he was, and he kept the sun's position in mind as he followed a course to the camp.

About a hundred yards to the south, Mark, Penny, and David began their own trek. They too had questioned what they had to do.

"We've got to get weapons if we can," Mark said, "and free Keno's men if they're being held. Then we need to radio Cairo or use the fax."

"If we can't get to the radio or the fax, we'll have to grab one of the cars and get away," David said.

"What's that smoke coming from?" Penny asked, pointing to the south.

The boys looked and saw the dirty plume reaching into the sky, bent westward by the desert wind.

"That's from burning fuel," Mark observed.

"We'd better keep a lookout in all directions," David said grimly. "Something's happened." But they could only guess at what it was.

They discussed the best way to enter the camp and decided, finally, to approach the southern edge and then come to the workers' trailer from the west.

"They shouldn't be expecting anyone from that direction," David reasoned. "Since they were following us in the underground passage, they'd all be looking toward the Nile for us. Coming from the opposite side of the camp, we'll catch them where they're not expecting trouble or keeping a lookout. I hope!" he added fervently.

"I'm soaked through!" Penny said, wringing water from the ends of her hair. Their clothes clung to them, dripping with river water. Their shoes sloshed when they walked, oozing water with each step.

"It won't take long for this hot sun to dry us out," Mark observed. "We'll be dry before we get to the camp."

"Let's go, then," David said, "and let's stay low between the dunes, so we won't be seen from a distance. I'll go ahead. If I'm seen, you two can hide."

Mark saw the wisdom in separating so that a car coming over the hill suddenly wouldn't catch all of them at once. David led the way, walking toward the camp between the sand dunes. When he'd gone about a hundred yards ahead, Mark and Penny followed.

It was not easy trooping through the soft sand in their wet shoes. Before long, though, their clothes began to feel dry—just as Mark had said.

"How long will we have to walk, Mark?" Penny asked as they struggled through the soft terrain. She'd put her camera case on her back, while he'd put the things from her other pack in his and strapped it on.

"I'm not sure," he replied. "It can't be far though. I know we'd planned to drive over to take pictures of the Nile in a day or so, and Mr. Froede said it wouldn't take long."

"Not in a car, maybe! But walking's another matter!" she answered. Then she asked, "Is David getting too far ahead?"

"No. It's really a good idea to separate like this. If a car comes over the dunes and catches him, we'll still be free. If a car catches us, he'll have a chance. Let's just pray that no one catches *any* of us!"

A large bird of prey circling high above the desert noted four people struggling from the river across the sand: one lonely figure to the north, another to the south, and two behind him—all moving with one purpose, it seemed, toward the cluster of buildings less than two miles away. The bird flew elsewhere, looking for smaller game.

CHAPTER 19

THE ASSAULT ON THE CAMP

Hoffmann raged like a madman! The tunnel to the river was blocked by a pile of rock that reached to the ceiling. And the secret passage into the treasure room refused to budge. Again and again his strongest men had tried to open the small door behind the pharaoh's chariot wheel. Again and again they had failed.

"It's blocked from inside, I tell you," one of the men declared. "Maybe those kids didn't die in the falling rocks. Maybe they got into the treasure room and blocked the door."

"We must get into that room!" Hoffmann roared. "We've wasted an hour already!" He turned. "Ahmet! Run to the camp and bring some picks. We'll break this wall down. I know the door is here. Oh, and go by the office to see if there are any phone or fax messages."

Ahmet turned, took one of his men, and started back to the entrance. They crawled through the small hole in the wall, out the door, and went up the steep stairs to the outside as fast as they could move.

No sooner had they gone than Hoffmann announced, "I'm going to radio the barge! They've got all the equipment we need—including dynamite. I'll tell them to hurry with whatever it takes. We can't wait for dark." He too ran down the passage and headed up the stairs.

Out on the open desert, Froede moved very carefully. He'd seen the top of the radio antenna that marked the position of the camp, and he didn't want to be spotted by a lookout and captured again! Crawling from dune to dune and keeping very low, he approached the three mobile homes that lined the northern perimeter of the camp. His was on the near end, and that's where he would find his pistol.

There was no one in sight as he peered around the dune nearest to his quarters. Carefully he moved across the remaining yards of sand, stood up quickly, and limped into the mobile home.

No one was there! Pulling his keys from his pocket, he quickly unlocked his drawer, took out a holstered Browning 9mm automatic, and belted it around his waist. Lifting out the pistol, he pulled back the slide and chambered a round. *Now I'm in business!* he said to himself. He tossed Ahmet's empty revolver on his bed and stepped to the door. He peered out, looking over the camp. Then he searched the site from each window. No one was visible—not anywhere in the camp.

Could they all be underground? he asked himself. He decided they had to leave someone on guard, and they had to leave someone at the radio. Therefore the office was the place to go. He stepped out the door and down to the sand, then limped purposefully to the office just twenty feet away. He prayed that his ankle wouldn't give way before he rescued the kids.

The scene inside the trailer was one of utter peacefulness and serenity. Ahmet sat at the desk facing the radio, while one of his men slouched in a chair beside him. Obviously neither expected trouble to come through the door.

Trouble came like a meteor. The guard beside Ahmet saw Froede first and jumped up, reaching for his rifle leaning against the wall. Froede hit him from behind, and the man lay still.

Ahmet turned, saw the battered Froede coming for him, and cried out in fear as he rose, knocking over the chair. He reached frantically behind him for a gun, but Froede was too fast. He simply shoved the tall traitor to the floor.

Ahmet quivered in fear. Froede knelt, placed the Browning at close range, pressed one knee on Ahmet's chest, and said very quietly, "Now you're going to tell me what you've been up to."

Ahmet looked into the blazing eyes of his deadly serious employer and began to tell him everything he knew.

Just minutes later, on the other side of the cluster of mobile homes, David and Mark entered the quarters of the workers, looking for weapons. They found instead two men on the floor, hands and feet tied, mouths sealed with tape. Mark stepped to the door and waved for Penny to join them.

"These men are loyal, Mark," David observed, "or they wouldn't be tied."

"Let's cut them loose," Mark replied. The boys found a knife from the kitchen unit and freed the men.

They gasped for air and struggled to rise. Pain shot through them as the blood returned to their limbs. There was anguish in their faces as they told the boys of Ahmet's deception, of Froede's and Keno's capture, and of the invading Jeeps with their loads of dangerous men.

"Mr. Froede and Keno got away in one of the vans! And one of the Jeeps went after them! That's when they tied us up!"

"So they got away!" Mark replied. The youngsters were thrilled at this news.

"That makes things simpler, Mark," David said quickly. "Let's see if we can shut those guys in the tomb. Then they'll be penned up until we can call for help!"

"Great idea!" Mark agreed. He turned to the men they'd cut loose.

"Have you got any guns here?" Mark asked.

"Keno has," one of the men replied. "He has two pistols." He stumbled to his feet and walked unsteadily toward Keno's chest of drawers. Here he pulled out two guns, a large and a small revolver, and handed one each to Mark and David. Both guns were loaded.

"Fine!" said Mark, as he took the smaller revolver

and handed it to his sister. "Penny, you stay here. Watch the door. Don't let anyone in unless it's Keno or Mr. Froede. Tell anyone else who tries that you'll shoot if they don't stop. If they keep coming, shoot. We'll head for the tomb entrance and see if we can find Mr. Froede and Keno."

She took the gun, too scared to object. "Remember," Mark said, "shoot anyone who forces his way into this mobile home. Dad taught you how."

She nodded silently and looked at Mark and David in turn. "You guys, please be careful!"

"Don't worry," Mark replied. "We will! And we'll be right back."

The four men left the mobile home and headed at once for the tunnel steps that led to the tomb.

"Be quiet!" David warned. Pistol in hand, he led them down the steep steps. Step by step they descended, careful to make no sound. At the bottom they paused, but no one was in sight, nor did they hear anyone. Silently the four of them moved to the heavy tomb door, pulled it away from the wall, and shoved. Once again the massive stone door slammed shut with the sound of an explosion! The shock wave reverberated down the entrance hall, into the small side room, and down the passage to the men struggling to crash into the treasure room of the pharaoh.

On the desert above, the one remaining able-bodied man from Curt's burned Jeep had finally staggered back to the camp. His tan shirt and blue jeans were burned and torn. His blond hair was ragged and singed on one side. Burned on his arms, thirsty, tired, and mad as a wild bull, he barged through the door of the first mobile home in his path, desperate for a drink.

He found instead a frightened young girl with a pistol in her hand pointed at his belt!

"Don't come any closer!" Penny said. Her voice quavered—but her pistol did not.

This was too much! The burly fighting man wasn't going to be stopped by a girl, not after what he'd been through. The long walk in the sun had burned his face a bright red, but his anger made it redder still. He spoke, and she recognized at once that he was an America.

"Now what's a pretty little girl like you doing with a great big gun like that?" The man sneered and kept coming toward her, reaching out for the gun in her hand.

Aiming deliberately above his head, Penny squeezed the trigger. The noise of the gun reverberated in the narrow room. Stunned, the man stumbled backward, tripped at the door, and fell sprawling to the sand below.

Hoffmann was in his Jeep, speaking to the barge captain by radio. "We need tools, one of your tractors, and maybe some dynamite," he said quickly, sketching the situation in the blocked passage as rapidly as he could. They were about to conclude when Hoffmann heard the awful unmistakable sound of the tomb door slamming shut.

He dropped the radio receiver in surprise and looked out the window of the Jeep. That's why he didn't hear the sudden cries of the barge captain over the phone: "Helicopters! They're coming straight at us! Hoffmann! Helicopters are attacking us!"

Hoffmann didn't hear the words. But he did hear the sound of Penny's pistol! He whipped his head to the left in time to see one of his men crash out the door of a mobile home and collapse on the desert sand!

Hoffmann pulled his gun and started to get out of the Jeep when he suddenly saw a man step out of another mobile home. From pictures he'd studied, he knew it was Froede!

How'd he get away from Curt and his men? Hoffmann asked himself in shocked surprise. He turned his pistol toward Froede; but then, in the corner of his vision, saw four figures dash up from the steps to the tunnel and spread out into the space before the mobile homes. One had a pistol.

These were not his men! His mind reeling with shock, Hoffmann cowered low in the seat of the Jeep. He had to figure this out!

The sleek white helicopter streaked low over the sand and hovered just long enough for two men to jump to the ground. Then it dashed across the site, dropped two more men, and landed between two of the mobile homes. All the men had submachine guns and fanned out to cover the compound.

Hoffmann was a tactician. He was also a realist. He

was, in fact, a realistic tactician who knew when the fight was lost. Without a moment's hesitation he turned the key in the ignition, stepped on the accelerator, and eased the Jeep into motion, turning behind the last mobile home to keep out of sight of the helicopter and Froede. Then he stepped on the gas and took off for the river!

CHAPTER 20

THE MOP-UP

The barge captain was elated! He was in touch with Hoffmann at last, the men were at the tomb, and he could stop this charade of moving up and down the river. Now he could get the job finished. He listened carefully as Hoffmann explained his need for tools to smash open the door to the treasure.

The two Egyptian helicopters arrived over the barge simultaneously, one from the east, the other from downriver. The first one streaked low over the desert, crossed the water, and hauled up suddenly to face the barge. It moved sideways with the craft—its cannons aimed directly at the captain on the bridge!

The other chopper came straight for the bow, hovered briefly with its cannon also aimed at the bridge, and settled gently down toward the deck of the barge. The lookout at the bow screamed in alarm, waved frantically at the helicopter, and then threw himself into the Nile.

On the bridge of the barge, the captain was equally alarmed. "Stop! You fools!" he screamed desperately at the descending chopper, his mind filled with visions of a crashed and exploding helicopter sending them all up in flames. Snatching his black cap from his head, he waved frantically at the approaching helicopter. "Stop! Stop!" he screamed again.

The helicopter did not stop. It landed on the deck of the barge, releasing a dozen armed, khaki-clothed men. They raced to cover the boat while a bearded, weather-beaten sergeant led a team of three to the bridge. No one on board dared resist. The lieutenant called from the deck, "All secured, Sergeant?"

"Yes, sir," the sergeant replied.

"Gas'm!" the lieutenant commanded.

Men moved to various vents on the tug and tossed tear gas grenades into the compartments below. Then they took up positions above the gangways and passageways, guns at the ready.

In moments, the gasping, coughing men struggled up from the spaces below. Quickly they were secured and handcuffed—all two dozen of them!

Less than a mile away now, a Jeep raced across the desert. Hoffmann knew he had escaped! The helicopter's men were too busy at the tomb site to bother with chasing him! Congratulating himself, he directed the bouncing Jeep across the uneven sand, around dunes, over unexpected piles of rocks. He was an expert driver; the path ahead gave him no fright at all. He'd get to the river, jump on the barge, and ride away in safety. He began to think of those three kids—they'd robbed him again!

He flew across another dune at great speed and

stood suddenly on the brakes! A helicopter was hovering over the barge, its nose pointed at the bridge. Another chopper was parked on the deck. The barge had been captured! His escape was gone!

Cursing viciously, Hoffmann swerved the Jeep, slowed down to lessen the trail of sand kicked up by its wheels and wind, and headed back behind the low hills. He had to get out of sight of those choppers! Gradually his heart slowed to normal. He'd made it again!

He laughed out loud and stepped on the gas. The land suddenly sloped upward, so he increased speed even more. Heading up as he was, he could not see the deep indentation of the Nile into the ground ahead of him. The Jeep roared off the cliff at top speed, curved gracefully in a long arc, then hurtled directly toward the Nile below.

Back at the camp, Paul Froede hugged Penny. "Oh, Uncle Paul, we didn't know what had happened to you!"

"I didn't know what had happened to *you*," he replied, now hugging her with one arm while gripping first Mark's hand, then David's with the other.

"Foucachon and André are in the tunnel, Paul," Chastain said. "The others are rounding up the survivors, but there's a gang inside the tomb, they're trying to push open that stone door. It seems to be too heavy." He smiled knowingly!.

"It *is*, rather," Froede agreed. "But don't spoil their

game. Let them have their exercise." He grinned his impish grin.

The four Egyptian helicopters arrived simultaneously from the four points of the compass in an incredibly precise assault. Two covered the site with their guns; two unloaded troops armed with assault rifles and submachine guns. Froede's men held up their guns in prearranged salute. The troops waved and headed for the various mobile homes and the tomb door.

The Egyptians hadn't lost a thing from the tomb.

CHAPTER 21

TO PARIS!

Mark, Penny, and David flew back to Cairo with Froede in the white helicopter, leaving Froede's men to secure the site with the Egyptian forces. As the chopper soared low over the desert, Froede told them what he'd learned.

"This was an incredible plot!" he said in grudging admiration. "The same guys who bribed Sanderson in your Dad's office in Africa bought Ahmet's soul here. Sanderson had learned from my communications with your Dad that we were on to something in Egypt, and he told his bosses. They planned this at least a year ago—that's when Ahmet said he was bribed—and have been waiting ever since."

He shook his head as the swift craft raced above the sand to the airfield outside of Cairo. "Their plan was to capture all of us as soon as we discovered the passage to the treasure room, force more information from Keno and me, steal the treasure, and leave us to die in the building underground. They'd shut us in—as if it were an accident—and let us suffocate."

He frowned at the thought of how close Hoffmann's men had come to pulling it off. "The treasure was to be

142

taken through the tunnels to the river. A hole would be blasted through the rock if they couldn't get the original door open. They'd move the treasures by barge down the river and load them on a fleet of trucks a couple of nights later. Ultimately, they'd be loaded on two freighters and taken to the Far East. Then they'd be sold on the international black market for hundreds of millions of dollars!"

"But who was behind all this, Uncle Paul?" Penny asked. "All those people and all those arrangements took a lot of money. Who's been paying for this all these years?"

"The former KGB and the East German Security Police," he replied. "When their governments collapsed a few years ago, many of their people went underground. These renegades haven't given up," he said grimly, "though their governments have disowned them. They still have a worldwide network built up for the past seventy years or so—but they do need money."

He looked at Mark and Penny in turn. "That's why our firm looked so attractive to them. Your Dad had found that diamond field in Africa; we found this tomb in Egypt. They thought their penetration of our work would bring them *two huge hauls*, each worth hundreds of millions of dollars!

"And it would have—if you kids hadn't spoiled their game! You blocked them in Africa, and you've blocked them here. But the Lord knows," he added sadly, "your Dad and I would never have put you into these dangers if we'd had any idea at all of what was going on." His eyes looked bleak.

"We know that, sir," David said. "None of us knew what was going on. My folks wouldn't have let me visit Mark and Penny for a 'peaceful vacation' if they'd thought any of this would happen! But the Lord knows what He's planned for all of us, doesn't He?"

"He does, indeed, David," Froede agreed, "He does, indeed!"

"Mr. Froede, I'm still puzzled about something," David said, a frown on his face. "What made you show me the way out of the tomb? If you hadn't done that, Hoffmann's men would have captured us."

"I saw a worker with Ahmet that I'd never seen before," Froede replied. "Just for a minute—he ducked out of sight as soon as he saw me. But I knew then that they'd brought in someone else and that I had to warn you."

"What about Hoffmann?" Mark asked. "Did they get him?"

"Not yet," Froede paused a moment before he continued. "He drove off in the Jeep just as the helicopters arrived. He was last seen near the barge, but when he saw it had been captured he turned and went downriver. After that, his Jeep just disappeared, though we sent a helicopter to search for it." He frowned, clearly puzzled. "It really did—it just disappeared. But he's certainly out of your lives. His teams are captured and his vehicles as well. The whole network is gone. You'll never see that man again!"

Five days later, Penny was to remember those words. But now she was exhausted. She leaned back against the seat, then rested her head on David's shoulder. He smiled and put his arm around her. She closed her eyes and was soon fast asleep.

Froede grinned, winked at David—whose face reddened!—then leaned back in his seat beside Mark. He closed his eyes also. He'd taken a quick shower at the camp and changed clothes. He would need several days for his ankle and bruises to heal.

After their rescue, Froede had asked them to pack all their things while he showered. "You've done far more than anyone could have asked," he said gratefully, "and while there's plenty to be done here at the tomb, I think it's time for a change. Time to get you out of here! We're going back to Cairo." No one had objected.

They slept until the helicopter landed at the airfield where Froede bundled them in his car. He refused Mark's offer to drive, took the wheel himself, and headed for the city.

"Remember, try not to alarm my wife—or your mother, Penny!" he said as he drove them to his house. "I'll call your folks and let you talk to them. Tell them you'll write at once with some details. I'll have to find out from the colonel what details we can mention."

When they arrived at Froede's house, his wife, Joan, welcomed them with open arms. She didn't seem very surprised at her husband's cuts and bruises. She told him to go to the bathroom and get out some medications and she'd be right there to doctor his cuts.

"You young folks shower and put on some decent clothes," he called as he left the room. "Jackets and ties, boys! I'm taking everyone out to a fabulous restaurant for dinner. I've also got some interesting news. Will an hour and a half give you enough time to get ready for dinner, young lady?"

"I'll try to make it, Uncle Paul!" Penny laughed.

By the time they'd showered, dressed, and driven back in to the city, it was a fashionably late hour at which to dine! They dined at the fabulous Justine's, one of the finest restaurants in Cairo.

Froede had finished his plate and the youngsters were almost through with theirs, but his wife was eating slowly. The specialty was lamb, and the Americans loved it.

"Joan," he asked in surprise, "don't you like the lamb?"

"I love it! But, Paul, you know I never eat this much!" She looked closely at his face as she'd been doing throughout the meal. "You really banged yourself up this time, didn't you? What in the world did you do to get all those cuts and bruises?"

"Oh, I'll tell you all about it later. Isn't anyone interested in my news?"

"What news?" Penny asked eagerly. Then she bit her lip. She had not forgotten, but she wasn't going to let him think she was curious. Now she couldn't restrain herself. "What news, Uncle Paul?" she repeated, since he hadn't answered.

"Well, there are many things ahead," he mumbled.

"Paul, stop teasing Penny and tell them the news. You're tantalizing them." Joan insisted. She shook her head in wonder. "You are really the limit sometimes—like right now!" She smiled at the kids.

"Oh, all right, he said, putting his napkin on the table. "Everyone's in such a rush. Life's really too short to rush things like this."

"But you're the one who asked *us*, Uncle Paul!" Penny replied. "That's not fair!"

"All right! All right! I'm ready!" he announced. "Well, you three have done the work we asked you to do here. You've done a great deal more, in fact." This he said with great seriousness, looking at each of them in turn. Clearly he was pleased.

"Your folks and I thought we could use you on one more job. But this time it will be more of a vacation. Mark and Penny, your parents are flying to Paris in two days. Your Dad's got to meet with the people we work for. They'll be there a couple of weeks and they want you three to join them."

He turned to David. "We've called your folks and they think that's fine. They want you to call them tomorrow, to check in."

The three almost shouted their surprise, "Paris!"

"Not so loud! Please!" he looked around at the other tables, pretending to apologize for the noisy teenagers.

Then he continued outlining the plan. "You'll fly to Paris day after tomorrow. It'll be a kind of vacation. What do you think?"

They were ecstatic.

Later that night, the three of them walked round and round the Froedes' yard under a golden half moon. Penny, lovely in her light blue dress walked between the two boys. Her left hand held her brother's strong arm. David held her other hand in his.

Already their minds were on the fabled city of Paris! The jewel of Europe, center of Western civilization, center of culture and art, the City of Light! They could hardly believe it. What a pleasant and relaxing time they'd have there!